"THAT'S HER!" HE SAID, GRABBING FOR HIS GUN.

"You're dead," Wade said.

"Wade, don't—" his brother said, but there was no stopping him.

Scarlet had no choice but to fire.

"Damn it!" Grafton said, but he was smart enough not to draw his gun. Instead he looked at the man and said, "Who the hell are you?"

"My name is Adams, Clint Adams."

Grafton gaped. "The Gunsmith?"

"That's right."

"Aw, damn," Grafton said.

Also in THE GUNSMITH series

THE GUNSMITH

118

SCARLET FURY

J. R. ROBERTS

JOVE BOOKS, NEW YORK

SCARLET FURY

A Jove Book / published by arrangement with
the author

PRINTING HISTORY
Jove edition / October 1991

ISBN: 0-515-10691-7

Jove Books are published by The Berkley Publishing Group,
200 Madison Avenue, New York, New York 10016.
The name "JOVE" and the "J" logo
are trademarks belonging to Jove Publications, Inc.

PROLOGUE

Her name was Scarlet, and she was looking for a man.

Oh, not the way other women look for men. She wasn't looking for one to take her to the spring dance, or to court her, or even to marry her. She was looking for a man . . . to kill.

It wasn't just any man, though. Oh, she didn't know his name, but she would know him when she saw him. Once there were five men like that, five nameless men who had raped her when she was sixteen and killed her whole family. She had killed the other four already. It had been a few years since the deaths of the third and fourth men, and she was still looking for the fifth.

As she rode into Ralston, Texas, she was actually looking for four brothers who had a price on their head. To finance her seemingly never-ending search for her mysterious fifth man, she had taken to hunting men for bounty. The only skill she had was with a gun, and it was a skill she had put long hours into perfecting. She was very good with a gun, so good that there were few— men or women—who were better. She knew a man who was better than she was with a gun, but she hadn't seen Clint Adams in years. It was odd to her that their paths hadn't crossed again since that first time together.

The brothers were the Grafton boys, four vicious men

who made their living robbing and killing. She had been trailing them for a month, but the collective bounty on their heads would make the time well spent. Meanwhile, while she trailed them, she kept her eye out for that fifth man.

She rode to the livery and, ignoring the appreciative glances of the liveryman, left her horse there and walked to the hotel. Appreciative glances were something you became used to when you were twenty-six, tall, full-bodied, with flaming red hair that fell halfway down your back. Glances, and advances, were things she had learned long ago how to deal with.

The one thing about having all that flaming red hair, though, was that people remembered you. Even if they forgot the beautiful face and figure, they remembered that flaming red hair.

"You sure it was her?" Wade Grafton asked.

"Sure I'm sure," Harley Grafton said. "She's got all that red hair, remember?"

"Lots of women have red hair," Wade said.

"Lots of women don't wear a gun," Harley said.

"She's still doggin' our trail, after all this time?" Wade said, shaking his head.

"I guess so," Harley said. "What are we gonna do, Wade? We got to meet up with Lee."

"We'll meet up with Lee," Wade said, "after we take care of this woman—what's her name?"

"She ain't got a name."

"Whataya mean she ain't got a name?" Sam Grafton asked from the corner.

All three Grafton brothers were sharing a room at the second of Ralston's two hotels. Wade, at fifty, was the oldest. Harley was thirty-five, and Sam twenty-nine. The leader, however, was Lee, who was forty-four. Wade knew that Lee was the smartest, and had long ago accepted it. After all, it was Lee who planned all their jobs.

Lee had a job planned now, and had sent for his three brothers to help pull it off. Before they met with Lee, however, they were going to have to take care of this nuisance.

"Everybody's gotta have a name," Sam said.

"Well, I heard she calls herself Scarlet."

"Scarlet?" Sam said.

"That's appropriate," Wade said.

"Huh?" Sam said, not understanding.

"It's fitting."

"Why?" Harley asked.

"That's gonna be the color of her blood, after we fill her full of holes."

Scarlet registered at the hotel. She signed in as "Scarlet," and under "residence" she wrote "none." She was staying in the other hotel in town, which was across the street from the one the Graftons were staying in. Harley Grafton had been on his way out of his hotel when he saw Scarlet walking down the street. He had ducked back into the lobby and watched her until she entered the hotel across the street. Then he'd hurried back up to his room to tell his brothers.

Scarlet went to her room and thought for a moment about a bath. She dismissed it with a shake of her head, dropped her saddlebags and rifle on the bed, and left the room. She started off down the street and stopped at the first restaurant she saw. She had a steak with vegetables, left the restaurant, and stopped at the first saloon she saw. She had half of a beer, left, walked down the street, and stopped at the next saloon she saw. At every stop she examined the faces of every man in the room without their realizing it. She also fended off at least one advance per place. She had learned how to do so without offending the man making the advance, so she wouldn't have to deal with a wounded ego. Men with wounded egos often became violent. She never again wanted to kill a man simply because she had wounded his male pride.

Halfway through the beer at the second saloon she asked the bartender, "How many other saloons are there in this town?"

"A couple," he said, leaning on the bar with his elbows, "but you belong right here, lady."

"Why is that?"

"Because in five more minutes I'm gonna ask you to marry me, and then this place will be half yours." The bartender was fifty, and fat.

She looked around, as if studying the place, and then patted him on the arm. "I'll be back after I check out the other places."

He smiled and said, "I'll be here."

"What is she doin' hopping from one saloon to the other?" Sam Grafton asked.

"What do you think she's doin'?" Wade Grafton asked. "She's lookin' for us."

"When is she gonna find us?" Harley asked.

Wade smiled and said, "Soon, very soon."

She had half a beer in the third saloon, and then left to find the fourth.

The fourth saloon was in what was usually referred to as the "red light" district. Most towns had them, and there was usually a "line" that separated this part of town from the "decent" part of town.

Scarlet stepped over the line, and the Graftons were waiting for her.

ONE

"You get yourself into more trouble reading the newspaper," Rick Hartman said to Clint Adams.

Clint was sitting across the table from Rick in Rick's Labyrinth, Texas, saloon.

"Huh?"

"You invariably see something in the newspaper that sends you off to some town somewhere to see if you can't help somebody from your past."

"Hmm?"

"Of course, I realize that you have a lot of friends and acquaintances from the past, given all the traveling you've done. I mean, I count myself among your friends, and sometimes I wonder what my life would have been like if I had chosen to travel instead of settling down and becoming a businessman."

"Uh-huh."

"I mean, I'm really more of an entrepreneur than a businessman, don't you think?"

"Mmm-hmm."

"I guess I'll leave here one of these days, but not until I can go to someplace like San Francisco and open the kind of gambling hall I'd really like to own."

"Sure."

"What is it you're finding so interesting in that paper?" Rick asked.

"An article."

"On what?"

"Guns."

"I should have guessed," Hartman said. "There are only two things in the world that you like."

Clint lowered the paper and frowned at his friend. "Guns and what?"

"Girls," Hartman said, "women . . . ladies, guns and females, those are your two main interests in life."

Clint frowned again, considering his friend's remarks carefully.

"I don't think I can argue with that," he finally said, and lifted the newspaper again.

"I wasn't looking for an argument," Hartman said to the other side of the newspaper, "just some conversation."

"What?"

"Never mind," Hartman said. "Do you know you're reading yesterday's paper?"

Again Clint lowered the paper and looked at his friend, then at the date on the paper.

"It was on the table when I got here," Clint said.

"That doesn't make it today's paper."

Clint folded the paper and put it down on the table. "Have you got a copy of today's newspaper?"

"You mean you're not going to finish that one?" Hartman asked, indicating the paper on the table.

"That's yesterday's news," Clint said. "I'd rather read today's."

"Don't you know," Hartman said, "that today's paper

always carries yesterday's news? I mean, that's the very nature of a newspaper. That one," he said, inclining his head to indicate the paper on the table again, "has the news of two days ago."

"Fine," Clint said. "Do you have a copy of today's paper, which has yesterday's news?"

"There's probably one around here somewhere," Hartman said.

Clint picked up his coffee, sipped it, and then put it down with a face.

"Cold," he said.

"Sure it is," Hartman said. "You've had your nose buried in that newspaper for the past twenty minutes. I'm surprised you finished your breakfast before starting to read."

"I was hungry."

The saloon was empty, except for a bartender at the bar and Hartman and Clint at the table eating breakfast. Theirs was the only table that didn't have the chairs upturned on its surface.

Hartman waved at T.C., the black bartender, and said, "Hot coffee for his highness."

"Comin' up," T.C. said. He had been reading a newspaper at the bar, and put it down so he could bring over the coffeepot.

"That today's paper you're reading?" Clint asked as T.C. poured their coffee.

"Yep."

"Anything interesting?"

"As a matter of fact," T.C. said, "there is. Some news out of Ralston."

"Ralston?" Hartman said. "That's a day's ride west of here, isn't it?"

"I guess," T.C. said.

"What's so interesting?" Clint asked.

"You ever heard of the Grafton brothers?"

"Who hasn't," Clint said. "They're wanted in six or seven states, including Texas."

"Well, seems two of them got themselves killed in Ralston . . . by a woman."

"A woman?" Hartman asked. "See?" he said to Clint. "Women can kill you."

"Well, this one did it with a gun," T.C. said, "in a street shooting."

"Really?" Hartman said, interested. "How did that come about?"

"Seems the woman was hunting them for the bounty on their heads," T.C. said. "The three of them attacked her in the street."

"And she killed two of them?" Hartman asked. "What about the third?"

"He got away."

"And the woman?"

"Took a bullet."

"Serious?"

T.C. frowned and said, "It don't say."

"What was the woman's name?" Hartman asked.

"It don't say," T.C. repeated.

"Does it describe her?" Clint asked. He had been listening intently. He knew a few women who might find themselves in that situation, including three lady bounty hunters—Anne Archer, Sandy Spillane, and Katy Littlefeather—who worked together.

"Said something about red hair," T.C. said. " 'Flaming red hair,' it said."

Clint stood up, walked to the bar, picked up the paper,

located the story, and started reading it.

"What's wrong with him?" T.C. asked.

Hartman stared over at his friend, and then said to T.C., "His coffee's going to get cold again."

TWO

When Clint Adams rode into Ralston, Texas, the shooting incident he'd read about in the newspaper was only four days old. He hoped that the woman in the story—who he thought was the woman he knew as "Scarlet"—hadn't yet left town. The newspaper had given no indication of the seriousness of her injury. For all he knew, she might even be dead by now, but he was holding his breath that this wouldn't be the case.

He left Duke, his big black gelding, at the livery and asked the liveryman what he knew about the red-haired woman who had been involved in the shooting four days ago.

The man's eyes lit up.

"I ain't never seen a woman who looked like that before in my life," the man said. Since he was in his sixties and had had himself a fairly long life, that was saying a lot. It also made Clint even more sure that the woman was Scarlet.

"Is she still in town?"

"Far as I know," the man said. "Leastways, her horse is still here."

"Can I see it?"

The man squinted and asked, "Why should I let you?"

"You're right," Clint said, "you shouldn't. Forget I asked."

"You a friend of hers?" the man asked as Clint was in the act of leaving.

Clint turned back and said, "If it's the woman I'm thinking about, yes."

"Hair like fire?"

"That's right."

"Blue eyes?"

"No," Clint said, shaking his head, "green. Tall and well built. That her?"

The man grinned, revealing gaps where teeth used to be, and said, "That's her, all right. Come on, I'll show you her horse."

The man walked Duke along with them until they reached a stall about halfway in.

"That's her mare," he said. "I'll put your horse in the next stall."

"Much obliged," Clint said.

While the man tended to Duke, Clint moved into the stall and looked the mare over. She wasn't overly large, but she was well muscled. This wasn't the same horse Scarlet had had the last time he saw her, but that didn't mean anything. Not everyone had a horse as long as Clint Adams had had Duke.

"That her horse?" the man asked.

"Can't tell," Clint said. "You know what hotel she's staying in?"

"There's only two, so she shouldn't be too hard to find."

"I expect that means she wasn't killed in that shoot-out?"

"Naw," the man said. "I heard she took a bullet in her arm."

"Okay," Clint said, accepting his saddlebags and rifle from the man, "thanks. Take good care of my horse."

"Animal that good-looking? You can bet I'll take care of him."

Clint had faith in the man. He had the scarred hands of a man who had been taking care of horses all his life, and Clint liked the idea that he hadn't been so willing to let him take a look at Scarlet's horse—if it *was* Scarlet's horse.

"Again," he said, "thanks."

He left the livery and went in search of the two hotels.

He found Scarlet registered at the first hotel he came to. He registered himself and reversed the book so the clerk could look at it.

"What room is the lady Scarlet in?"

"The gun-totin' lady?" the clerk asked, his eyes lighting up. "Why should I tell you what room she's in?"

"So I don't go knocking on all the doors in your hotel bothering your guests, that's why?"

"I could call the sheriff."

"Call him," Clint said. "The lady is a friend of mine."

"Sure," the clerk said, "every man in town wants that to be true."

Clint had the feeling that Scarlet's experience had somehow endeared her to the hearts of the people of Ralston, Texas, so that they seemed intent on protecting her.

"All right," Clint said, "you've got no reason to believe me. Forget it."

"Forget it?" the clerk said, unsure that Clint was being sincere.

"I'll talk to the sheriff," Clint said. "Where can I find him?"

"His office is down the block," the clerk said, "end of the street."

"What's his name?"

"Carpenter," the clerk said, "Ed Carpenter."

"All right," Clint said, "thanks."

He went to his room, dropped off his gear, and then headed for the sheriff's office.

THREE

He found the sheriff's office with no problem. There was a wooden placard on the wall with the words ED CARPENTER, SHERIFF on it. He knocked on the door, and entered.

The man behind the desk looked up at him in surprise. Maybe nobody had ever knocked before entering before.

"You the sheriff?" Clint asked.

"I am. What can I do for you?"

Ed Carpenter was in his early fifties, and had been sheriff in Ralston for over twelve years. Before that he'd been a lawman in plenty of other towns, but he'd never found one he liked as much as Ralston. The people in this town treated each other with respect, and he hadn't run into that very often in other towns. Rather than compete with each other, the people of Ralston put all their efforts into making their town a decent place to live and raise children.

"I'm looking for a woman," Clint said.

"What woman would that be?"

"The one who was involved in a shooting four days ago? With the Grafton brothers?"

"What about her?" the sheriff said, giving Clint a suspicious look.

"Well, I'm trying to find out if she's the woman I'm thinking of. If she is, then she's a friend of mine and I'd like to know how she is."

"You wouldn't be here in behalf of the Grafton boys, would you?"

"No," Clint said, "I wouldn't. Sheriff, my name is Clint Adams. If the woman calls herself Scarlet, then she knows me. Everybody in this town seems to be trying to protect her—but there's no need to protect her from *me*."

"This town respects women," the sheriff said. "We don't take kindly to three men trying to gun a woman down in the street—not even a woman who can take care of herself."

"Look," Clint said, "if you'll tell her I'm here, I'm sure she'd want to see me."

Carpenter studied Clint for a few moments, then stood up. Seated, the man had looked slender, even bony, but when he stood he revealed a paunch that didn't go with the rest of his body.

"I'll take you to her," Carpenter said, "but if she don't want to see you, you're gonna have to leave."

"Fair enough."

"I know who you are, Adams," Carpenter said, "but I ain't afraid of you."

"That's good, Sheriff," Clint said, "I'm glad to hear it."

"Just so's you know."

The sheriff led the way out of his office and turned left.

"Aren't the hotels that way?" Clint asked.

"She ain't in either of the hotels," Carpenter said. "Just follow me."

Clint nodded, and followed the man in silence.

• • •

Sheriff Ed Carpenter led Clint to a house at the far end of town. Clint assumed that it was a boardinghouse. They mounted the front porch and Carpenter knocked on the door. It was answered by a man wearing a deputy's badge.

"Sheriff," the man said, with a nod. He looked past the sheriff to Clint.

"This man's with me, Bob," Carpenter said. He looked at Clint and said, "Come on inside."

They entered the house under the wary eye of the young deputy. He was taller than Clint, and about twenty years younger. He stood with his chest blown out and his thumbs hooked into his gunbelt. Clint couldn't remember being that young and cocky.

"Who is he?" the deputy asked.

"He says he's a friend of hers," the sheriff said.

"Sure," the deputy said, eyeing Clint suspiciously.

Carpenter led Clint into a sitting room and said, "Wait here."

Clint nodded, and the sheriff went upstairs, leaving Clint alone with the deputy. Clint sat on the divan and ignored the deputy.

"You best not be here to try and hurt her," the deputy said.

Clint turned his head and looked at the man. In addition to blowing out his chest and hooking his thumbs, the man had now stuck out his jaw. Clint figured he was trying to look ferocious, but he only succeeded in looking ridiculous.

"Like I said," Clint said, "I'm an old friend."

"Sure," the deputy said.

They waited in silence, and a few minutes later Clint

heard footsteps on the stairway. The sheriff came into sight first, and then the long legs of a woman, encased in boots and jeans.

Clint knew those legs.

"Scarlet," he said, even before her face and red hair came into view.

Scarlet stopped halfway down the stairs, staring at him.

"Clint," she said, finally, breathlessly, and hurried down the stairs to embrace him.

FOUR

As Clint hugged Scarlet to him, enjoying the feel of her firm body against his, he saw the deputy glaring at him and knew that Scarlet had herself another conquest. The young deputy was in love with her, and she probably didn't know he existed except for the badge on his shirt.

"Clint," she said again, hugging him tightly.

"I take it Adams is a friend of yours?" Sheriff Ed Carpenter said.

Scarlet pulled back so that she could look at Clint's face and replied without looking at the other man. "He's a very good friend."

Carpenter rubbed his jaw and stared at Clint.

"Do you mind if we have some privacy now, Sheriff?" Clint asked.

"Sure," Carpenter said, "sure."

He started for the door, but the deputy stood rooted to the spot, still glaring at Clint.

"And take your pup with you, will you?" Clint called after Carpenter.

Carpenter opened the front door and said, "Let's go, Bob."

"Yeah, but—"

"Bob!"

21

The young deputy glared at Clint one last time and then marched out the door. Carpenter nodded to Clint, and left, closing the door behind them.

"What's going on—" Clint started.

"What are you doing here—" Scarlet said at the same time.

"You first," Clint said.

"What are you doing here?"

Clint was about to answer, but he stopped and looked around them. "Do we have to talk here?"

"No, of course not," she said, taking his hand. "Come up to my room."

"What would your landlady say?"

"She's not around," Scarlet said, "so who cares."

As they walked up the stairs Clint wondered how a woman as beautiful as Scarlet could have gotten even *more* beautiful over the years. There was no longer any trace of "girl" in Scarlet. She was all woman. Her face was slimmer, her cheekbones more prominent, and if it was possible, her waist was slimmer, her breasts and hips fuller.

She led him down the hall to a room with an open door. Once inside, she closed the door and turned to face him. "Now tell me how you got here."

"I read about your shootout," Clint said, and explained how he had ridden over from Labyrinth, Texas, to see if the red-haired woman in the article was her.

"You knew it was me, didn't you?" she asked.

"I had a feeling," he said. "It's good to see you, Scarlet. I'm glad you're not seriously hurt."

"No," she said, looking at her left arm, lifting it slightly, "the bullet went right through."

"Tell me what happened," he said.

"After . . ." she said.

"After what?" he asked.

She smiled, unbuttoning her shirt, and said, "As if you didn't know . . ."

He explored her body with his hands and mouth. As he had suspected, her breasts had become fuller, as had her hips and thighs, and her waist was even more slender than it had been.

She was more than eager in bed, she was desperate. For years sex had been a weapon to her, and nothing more, as she hunted down the men who had raped her and killed her family. It was Clint who had showed her that sex was something to be treasured, and enjoyed—and she was enjoying it now.

She moved atop him, taking him inside of her, and rode him that way. Her head was thrown back, her hair trailing down her back and onto his thighs. He reached for her breasts and held them while she rode him, popping the nipples with his thumbs.

When she started to tremble he reached behind her and pulled her down so that she was flat against him. He ran his hands down her back to her firm buttocks and held her firmly to him while he emptied into her. . . .

"Oh God," she said, lying on her back next to him, "it's been a long time."

"Not that long," he said.

"No," she said, "not since the last time we were together, but pretty near. You damn near ruin a woman for any other men, Clint Adams."

"I'm sure there are some out there who could satisfy you," he said.

"Some," she said, "but none like you."

He leaned over and kissed her tenderly, her fingertips touching his cheeks until they broke the kiss.

"Now," he said, "tell me what happened."

"Well, I rode into town trailing the Grafton boys," she said. "I was looking for them, hopping from saloon to saloon. . . ."

When she had crossed the "line" into the "red light" district of Ralston, three of the Graftons had been waiting for her.

"Hello, missy," she heard a voice call, and she half turned to her right. The three of them stepped out of the shadows. She recognized them as Wade, Harley, and Sam.

"Where's Lee?" she asked.

Wade was the spokesman. "Lee leaves this sort of thing to us, missy."

"What sort of thing?" she asked. "Killing women? I heard Lee was pretty good at that."

"He is," Wade said, "but you're a special case, missy."

"Why's that?"

"You been on our trail for what? A month?"

"More?"

"More," Wade said. "I'll say this for you, you sure are persistent."

"Thanks," Scarlet said. "I'll take that as a compliment."

"You're also dead," Wade said, and she saw the three of them go for their guns.

Scarlet drew her gun and shot Wade first, hitting him in the shoulder. His shot went wild, and she moved her gun and fired at Harley, hitting him in the middle of the chest. Sam Grafton fired then, but hastily, and he missed. Scarlet shot him, and as she pulled the trigger she felt something strike her left arm. Wade had righted himself and fired at her, hitting her left arm. As he tried to fire again, however, his gun misfired, and he turned and ran. . . .

"Harley and Sam were dead," Scarlet said, "and I was bleeding like a stuck pig. I'd never been shot before, and I think I went into shock."

"You probably did," Clint said. "Lucky for you Wade's gun misfired."

"I guess," she said, frowning. "I should have had him too, though."

"Don't do that," Clint said. "You were facing three men, and one of them got lucky enough to wing you—and you managed to kill two of them and wound the third. You did more than anyone else—man or woman—could have done."

"You would have killed all three."

"Maybe," he said, "maybe not. There's no guarantee of that. Besides, you shouldn't be comparing yourself to me or anyone else."

"I know that," she said, "I'm just so damned mad at myself."

"Well, don't be." He took her into his arms, careful of her bandaged left arm, and kissed her. Her tongue snaked into his mouth and the kiss continued for a long time.

"Tell me how you happen to be here under protection of the law."

"I don't know," she said. "After the shooting the town just seemed to open up to me. Everyone's been so nice, and the sheriff insisted on giving me protection."

"Some protection," he said. "A lovesick deputy."

"Are you jealous?"

"Of him? Hardly."

"Well, you needn't be," she said. She kissed him again, and slid her hand between them to take hold of him. He rolled her over, once again mindful of her arm, and slid into her easily. She moaned, and wrapped her powerful legs around his waist.

"What do you intend to do now?" he asked, still later.

"You mean . . . right now?" she asked. Laughing, she used her right hand to clutch one of his buttocks.

"I mean now that you're almost recovered."

"Well, it's a lucky thing you got here when you did, or I would have missed you," she said. "I plan on leaving tomorrow."

"For where?"

"For wherever Wade Grafton's trail leads me—hopefully to his brother."

"For the money?"

"Hell, yes, for the money," she said. "I already collected on Harley and Sam, and I intend to collect on Wade and Lee."

"Do you need the money that badly?" he asked.

"I need the money, Clint," she said seriously. "You know why I need the money."

Indeed he did know why. She was still pursuing that fifth man from her past. Nine years or so had apparently done little to ease her thirst for revenge.

"Lee Grafton won't come easy, Scarlet."

"He might," she said, sliding her index finger along the crease between his buttocks, "if you were to come with me."

"Scarlet—"

"Just until this poor gal has a chance to heal properer?" she said, pouting. "You wouldn't want me facing Lee Grafton alone when I wasn't a hundred per cent, would you?"

She kissed his neck, and then his shoulders, moved her mouth down over his chest and belly, still downward. . . .

"You make an offer a man can hardly refuse," he said, reaching for her head.

FIVE

In the morning they left her room and walked to his hotel for breakfast. Outside her boardinghouse, as they left, Clint spotted the deputy Ed Carpenter had called Bob.

"There's your admirer," he said to Scarlet.

She looked, and also saw the man.

"That's sweet," she said. "Maybe we'd better tell the sheriff that we're leaving today."

"Sure," he said. "After breakfast. You sure know how to make a man work up an appetite, girl."

"I'm a little hungry myself," she admitted.

Wade Grafton woke with a start that morning. He looked around the room, not knowing where he was or how he had gotten there.

"You're awake," a woman's voice said.

He turned, and saw the woman entering the room with a tray.

"I know soup isn't the best breakfast in the world, but I figure it's what you kin handle right now."

The woman was in her forties, with an angular but not unattractive face, and a body to match. Her dark hair was caught in a bun behind her head.

"Who are you?"

29

"Are we gonna go through that again?" she asked, setting the tray on a small table next to the bed.

"What do you mean?"

"That's the third time in three days you've asked me that."

Wade frowned and said, "I don't remember. How did I get here?"

"I found you wandering around with a bullet in yer shoulder. You looked like you had traveled a good two days that way."

He looked down at himself, and realized that he was naked except for a bandage on his left shoulder. Wade Grafton had been shot and doctored enough over the years that he knew a professional job of bandaging when he saw one.

"I've done a lot of bandaging over the years," she said, as if reading his mind.

"And the bullet?"

"I took it out," she said. "I've done a lot of that too."

He used his right arm to push himself more upright so he could look around the room.

"Where am I?"

"My cabin," she said. "My home. I wasn't strong enough to carry you, so I drug you in."

"My horse?"

"It's outside, in my lean-to."

"How far are we from the Mexican border?"

"I figgered you was heading for Mexico," she said. "We're about half a day's ride. You almost made it before you fell off yer horse."

"I fell off my horse?"

"I found you wandering afoot," she said. "Found your horse an hour later. It hadn't gone all that far away."

"Why?" he asked.

"Why what?"

"Why did you bring me in?"

"You were hurt," she said, without hesitation. "I'd do the same for a hurt critter. You gonna eat some of this soup? If you're gonna keep runnin' you're gonna need your strength."

"What makes you think I'm running?"

"You mean you ain't?"

Wade didn't answer. He was wondering if he was going to have to kill this woman.

"It don't matter to me one way or the other," she told him. "Open yer mouth."

He obeyed and she spooned some soup in.

"Ugh," he said, "that's awful."

"I'm better at doctorin' than I am at cookin'," she admitted, "but at least it's hot, and it's good for you. Open."

He hesitated, then obeyed, and she spooned in some more.

"I'd better be leaving today," he said.

"Not today," she said. "Maybe tomorrow."

"It's got to be today," Wade said. "I'm meeting someone."

"They'll just have to wait."

"Look," Wade said, swinging his legs around so that he could put his feet on the floor, "I appreciate what you've done, but I gotta go."

She stared at him a moment, then moved out of his way and said, "Well, go ahead, then."

Wade stood up, and when he did the room suddenly turned sideways. He would have fallen if she hadn't taken hold of his arm and sat him back down.

"Satisfied?" she asked. "Now move yerself back up in that bed."

He did as she said, and when she said, "Open," he did that too.

"What's your name?" he asked, wiping a drop of soup from his chin.

She stared at him and said, "Now, I ain't asked you that, have I?"

"You afraid to tell me your name?"

"My name don't matter," she said, "and I don't wanna know yers."

"Why not?"

"The way I figger it," she said, "you're wonderin' now if yer gonna have to kill me or not. If I ask you yer name and you tell me, I figger you'll kill me fer sure. This way, I got a chance of livin'."

"You know all that and you're still helping me?"

She shrugged. "Like I said, I'd do the same for some hurt critter."

Wade stared at her, not knowing what to say next.

She lifted the spoon to his mouth and said, "Open."

Over breakfast Clint and Scarlet discussed what their route would be.

"What trail were you following that led you here?" he asked.

"I was simply traveling south, figuring that the Graftons were headed for Mexico."

"What do you think now?"

"I'm even surer now that Wade and his brothers were going to Mexico to meet with Lee," she said, pushing her plate away while there was still plenty of food left on it. "Wade will want to get there even more now, to tell Lee what happened to Sam and Harley."

"That means they'll be waiting for you," Clint said. "You must know that."

"Sure I know that," she said, "but they'll be waiting for *me* . . . not for *us*. I figure I've still got a pretty good edge."

"Maybe," Clint said.

"Why maybe?" she asked. She picked up a roll and bit into it.

"Do you have any idea how many men Lee has with him?" he asked.

She paused a moment in her chewing and said, "No, I don't."

"Did you figure that it would just be Lee and Wade we'd have to face?"

She frowned and said, "I guess not."

"No," he said, "I guess not too. Scarlet, no matter how many men Lee Grafton has with him, when he hears what happened to his brothers, he's going to get himself some more."

Scarlet's frown deepened, as if she were scolding herself for not realizing that.

"I wouldn't count on that edge being as good as you thought."

SIX

After breakfast Clint and Scarlet went to the sheriff's office, and found Ed Carpenter seated behind his desk, drinking coffee.

"Sheriff," Clint said, by way of greeting.

"You two heading out?" Carpenter asked.

"That's right," Clint said.

"Are you intending to trail Wade Grafton?" Carpenter asked, directing the question to Scarlet.

"Yes, I am," Scarlet said. "We're bound by lead, Sheriff. He left me some of his and I left him some of mine. We've got unfinished business."

"That's up to you, ma'am," Carpenter said. "I just feel it would be a damned waste if the Graftons up and killed you."

"That's sweet of you, Sheriff," Scarlet said, "but I'm not going alone."

Carpenter looked at Clint.

"That's right," she said. "Mr. Adams has agreed to ride with me . . . for a while."

"I see," Carpenter said.

"Sheriff, that deputy you call Bob?"

"Bob Kenilworth. What about him?"

"Do you get the feeling he's got some strong feelings about Scarlet here?"

Carpenter made a face and said, "He's young. He'll get over it."

"Well, I'd appreciate it if you made sure he didn't leave town to follow us."

"What makes you think he'd do a fool thing like that?" the sheriff asked.

"Sheriff," Clint said, "if you or I were that age, and thought we were in love with a woman like Scarlet, what would we do?"

Carpenter stared at his cup for a moment, then nodded and said, "I'll take care of it."

"Thanks."

"When are you leaving?"

"As soon as we collect our gear, and I check out of the hotel."

"Sheriff, I'll need to leave some money for Mrs. Mooney."

"Don't worry about that, ma'am," Carpenter said. "It's all taken care of."

"Sheriff, please—"

He held up a hand to silence her and said, "The town of Ralston insists on it, ma'am. You did us a service by making sure the Graftons didn't cause trouble in our town. We're beholding to you."

"Somehow," Scarlet said, "I think you've got that backwards, Sheriff."

When they left the sheriff's office they split up.

"Collect your gear from the boardinghouse," Clint said. "I'll check out of the hotel and meet you at the livery."

"All right."

Scarlet walked to the boardinghouse, entered, and walked up to her room. She entered, and had started collecting her gear when she felt someone else's presence in the room.

She turned and found the deputy, Bob, standing just inside the doorway.

"Deputy," she said.

The young man looked odd, uneasy, his eyes darting about the room, looking everywhere but at her.

"You can't leave," he said, still not looking at her.

"What's that?"

Finally, his eyes fell on her, and she saw two things in them. She saw a man who thought he was in love with her, and she saw a man who was beginning to lose control of himself.

"I said you can't leave," he said, nervously, "I—I won't let you."

"Now, Deputy—"

"My name is Bob," he said, cutting her off. "Can you say that?"

"Bob."

He smiled and said, "I knew it would sound like that when you said it."

"Bob," she said, again. "I have to leave."

She turned and collected her things, tossing some extra clothes into her saddlebags. She picked up her rifle with her left hand, and draped the saddlebags over her left forearm. It hurt some, but this left her right hand— her gun hand—free.

She turned and saw that Deputy Bob Kenilworth was still standing there. He was perspiring, and his eyes appeared glazed.

"Please," she said, "stand aside. I have to leave."

"With him?" he asked, vehemently.

"With who?"

"Adams, that's who," the deputy said. "You're leaving with him because he's got a big rep."

"I'm leaving with him because he's my friend, and he's going to help me."

"I can help you."

"Please . . ." She tried to slip by him, but he blocked her path. "Bob . . ."

"I love you."

"No, you don't."

"Yes, I do," he said, "and I won't let you go, Scarlet."

He reached for her and she backed off. She didn't like what she was seeing, in his face and in his eyes.

"Why are you backing away from me?" he asked. "I only want to love you."

She knew she was in trouble. She had to get by him without hurting him. The sheriff and the town had extended their hospitality to her, but if she hurt this young man, or killed him, their attitude would change quickly.

"Bob, listen to me—"

"If you don't stay," he said, "I'll kill you."

Now she knew she had to play it carefully. Clearly, Bob Kenilworth was a young man not in his right mind, and she knew better than to blame herself for that. She had driven men to a lot of things—yes, even to killing— but Kenilworth had problems of his own which were probably only now surfacing.

"Bob, listen to me," she said. "If you make a move against me, I'll have to kill you."

"I don't care," he said, close to tears now. "If I can't have you, I don't want to live."

His words were ludicrous, almost funny, but she could not afford to laugh—not now.

"All right, Bob," she said, moving closer to him. "All right."

"You mean . . . you'll stay?"

"Of course I'll stay," she said, moving closer still. "You don't think I want anything to happen to you, do you?"

"But—I thought you didn't even notice me."

"I didn't," she said, "but I'm noticing you . . . now!"

As she said the word "now!" she drew her gun and brought it down on his head, much too swiftly for him to react. He crumpled to the floor.

She stared down at him for a moment, then holstered her gun and left.

"I was going to come looking for you," Clint said as Scarlet entered the livery. He had already saddled Duke, and had just completed the saddling of her horse for her.

"Any problems?" he asked.

"No," she said, settling her saddlebags and rifle into place on her saddle and mounting up. "No problems."

He didn't believe her, but he didn't pursue the matter. He simply mounted up and said, "Then let's get moving."

SEVEN

They made good time and camped only once, just before dark. They dismounted and walked some periodically, to give the horses some rest, but Scarlet did not want to stop for any reason until nightfall.

They "chatted" during the day's ride, but to Clint's mind they never "talked." He knew there were things inside Scarlet that she never wanted to talk about, and he vowed to allow her to choose the subjects of their conversations. After all, he was there to help her, and he was asking nothing from her in return.

And that first day, nothing was just what he got.

Wade had been expecting her.

That is, he wasn't surprised when she came into the room, removed her robe, and got into bed with him—naked.

"I haven't had a man in a long time," she said.

He had noticed the way she'd been looking at him for most of that day. He pegged her for a man-starved spinster, and figured that was probably the real reason she had nursed him back to health.

"I won't hurt you," she whispered to him.

He had been lying naked in bed anyway, and she had to be the one who had undressed him, because there was no one else around.

"No," he said, "you won't."

She slid her hands down his body and took his manhood in both hands. Her flesh was hot, but as his hands moved over her he could feel the points of her bones, at the shoulders, at the hips. He could even feel every one of her ribs.

As she slid one leg over him he could smell her readiness. She came down on him, engulfing him in her slick, wet pussy, and her weight on him felt like nothing. He reached up and palmed her breasts, which were small and not particularly firm.

He had a choice, of course. He could have pushed her away, since she was not the kind of woman he would normally have sex with, but he figured, Why not? They were both there, she had hot skin and an ever hotter pussy, and in the dark she could be any woman he wanted.

She started to move on him, riding him up and down, and he pinched her nipples at the same time.

"Oh, yes, oh, Jesus, it's been so long . . . ooh, ooh, yes, yes . . ." She repeated that litany over and over, "Ooh, ooh, yes, yes . . ." as she continued to ride him, faster and faster. She was bouncing him on the bed, causing some discomfort to his shoulder, but not enough for him to protest. He closed his eyes and thought of a big-titted whore he'd known in Abilene, and before long he exploded inside of her, and she screamed.

When Scarlet woke the next morning she smelled the coffee and saw Clint sitting at the fire.

"How long have you been up?" she asked.

"Long enough to make the coffee."

She joined him at the fire, running her fingers through her hair to untangle it, then accepting a cup of coffee.

"I'm sorry," she said.

"For what?"

"I wasn't a very talkative traveling companion yesterday."

"You've got a lot on your mind."

"You're my friend," she said, "I should be talking to you, but . . ."

"It's been a while, Scarlet," he said, "and I'd be willing to bet you haven't confided in many people since the last time we saw each other."

"No," she said, laughing humorlessly, "none."

"I don't expect you to confide in me either," he said. "Not right away, anyway. I'm just here to help you."

"You are a good friend," she said. "Just give me a little time."

"Take all the time you need," Clint said.

"What's the next town?" she asked, changing the subject.

"Wilson Falls."

"How far are we from the border?"

"About three days' ride, if we push it."

"Let's push it."

"Duke is up to it," he said. "Is your mare?"

Now she smiled for real and said, "She'll keep up."

He dumped the remains of his coffee into the fire and said, "Then let's do it."

Wade woke the next morning with her lying on his good arm. He hadn't noticed it so much during the night, but he realized now that she needed a bath—and that he needed one as well.

He tried sliding his arm from beneath her without waking her, but she immediately opened her eyes and sat up, staring at him. Abruptly, she grabbed the sheet and pulled it up to cover her nakedness, conscious of her bony, skinny body.

"I, uh, better get breakfast," she said, not looking at him. She reached down next to the bed, got her robe, and stood up quickly to put it on. He saw her flat, shapeless buttocks and thin legs before she could cover them with the robe.

She left the room, still not having looked at him.

He thought about how eager she had been during the night, waking him twice more to fuck, talking dirty to him while they did it, and how now in the morning light she'd reverted to the prim and plain spinster of the day before.

He hadn't minded so much, but he wasn't sure he wanted to go through it all again, so he decided he was going to have to leave today—hopefully, within the hour.

He stood up, fought off the dizziness, took a step, and, heartened that he hadn't fallen down, took a second, and then a third . . . .

While Wade mounted up the woman watched him from her doorway. He knew he shouldn't leave her alive—and he'd never before been accused of sentiment—but he'd decided to let her live.

The reason escaped him just now, but it would come to him soon enough.

EIGHT

Lee Grafton was worried.

Well, he'd never admit that he was worried. The most he'd admit to would be . . . concern that his brothers hadn't yet arrived in the little Mexican town where he was waiting for them.

There wasn't much to do in the town of Domingo. Luckily, Lee had found Juanita. She was working in the tavern, and when he laid eyes on her, he took her out of there. He told her that he would pay her, and her only job was to make him happy.

At the moment, she was doing her best to do just that. Her head was bobbing up and down in his lap while he sat in a chair in his hotel room. He began to lift his hips to match the cadence of her sucking mouth when there was a knock on the door.

"Damn it!" he said.

She didn't stop, and he grabbed a handful of her dark hair and pulled her off him. "Answer the door, damn it!"

"*Sí*," she said. She welcomed the chance to spit him out of her mouth.

She walked to the door and opened it. When the man walked in Lee Grafton was pulling up his trousers.

"What do you want?" Lee demanded.

The man was staring at Juanita. Her peasant blouse had been pulled down so that her full, dark-nippled, pear-shaped breasts were bare. She gave the man a bold stare and slowly pulled the blouse back up to cover herself.

"Rock!" Lee said.

Sean Rock pulled his eyes from Juanita and looked at Grafton.

"Some of the men are getting pretty edgy, Lee," Rock said.

"Fuck them."

"Lee," Rock said, "if we don't do something soon, they'll ride out."

Grafton stared at Rock, who was essentially his second in command, and would be until his brothers arrived.

"Is that your observation, Rock, or have they said so?" he asked.

"Some of them have mentioned it."

"They won't leave," Grafton said confidently.

"How do you know?"

"Would you leave?"

"Well . . . no."

"Why not?"

"I'm loyal to you, Lee."

Grafton closed his eyes and said, "Give me another reason."

"Well . . . nobody plans jobs as big as the ones you plan."

"Then the reason is money, right?"

"Right."

"Money," Grafton said, "is the reason most of us do anything. Take Juanita here." Grafton approached

Juanita and pulled the peasant blouse down so that her dark breasts were once again exposed. He stroked one of them, lingering on the nipple. "She doesn't like me, but because I pay her enough she lets me do . . . this."

"Uh . . . yeah. I see."

"And this," Grafton said, cupping both of her breasts in his hands and lifting them, hefting their weight. Juanita stood stock still, no expression on her face while he continued to fondle her.

"Now, if I told her to moan in ecstasy, she would do that, too."

"Uh, yeah," Rock said, staring at Juanita's breasts.

Abruptly, Grafton took his hands away from her breasts. She made no attempt to cover herself this time.

"It's the same with the men, Rock," Grafton said. "They'll take whatever shit I dish out, because there's money in it for them at the end. Believe me, they won't leave."

"Uh, all right."

"Go and tell them that we aren't going to do a thing until my brothers get here."

"Okay."

"And tell them that anyone who has any objections should come and see me."

"O-okay."

Rock made no move to leave, but continued to stare openly at Juanita's naked breasts.

"Rock!"

"What?"

"Get out!"

"Right."

Rock turned and left the room, closing the door behind him.

Grafton unbuttoned his pants and lowered them. He wasn't wearing any underwear, and his penis was still fully rigid. He was a tall, bony man with thinning, sandy hair, large-knuckled hands, and a huge, heavily veined penis. Juanita thought it was the ugliest penis she had ever seen, especially on a man so thin.

"All right, Juanita," he said, smiling, "let's get back to it."

He sat in the chair, legs spread out.

She knelt between his legs, cradled his testicles in both her hands, and took him into her mouth. As she ministered to him, she thought only of the money that he gave her.

Lee Grafton was the only Grafton brother who had any kind of education. That was one of the reasons he was acknowledged as their leader, but it was by no means the only one.

Lee Grafton had a naturally gifted mind. His teachers had told him that in the Eastern schools he had attended—and yet, he'd chosen to direct his intelligence only towards illegal matters. He had worn out his welcome in the East with small-time robberies, and come West to rejoin his brothers. They'd been making a living robbing stagecoaches at the time, because their limited intelligence couldn't come up with anything bigger than that.

With Lee Grafton as their leader, they'd proceeded to pull bigger jobs, for a lot more money. Unfortunately, none of the brothers—not even Lee, with his superior intelligence—knew how to hold onto the money. They would invariably spend it all, and then Lee would plan another job, and the cycle would begin again.

That was what had happened now. Lee was out of money, and he was sure that his brothers were too. He had another job planned, probably the biggest of all. He had enough men with him in Domingo to pull it off, but he wasn't going to make a move until his three brothers arrived.

NINE

Clint and Scarlet left Wilson Falls the same day they arrived. There had been no sign that Wade Grafton had ever been there.

"He must have bypassed the town," Scarlet said as they were riding out.

"Let's remember that he was wounded," Clint said. "He might have been out of his head."

"But wouldn't he look for a doctor?"

"Not if he wasn't in his right mind," Clint said. "He could still be wandering aimlessly."

"Or he could be dead," Scarlet said. "How will we find him if there's no pattern to his path?"

"We'll just have to assume that he got help somehow, and that he's back on the trail to meet with his brother," Clint said. "It's the only course of action that makes any sense."

"I guess you're right."

"Don't get discouraged, Scarlet."

"I won't," she said. "I've been through too much to ever become discouraged."

When they camped at midday Scarlet brought up the subject of discouragement once again.

"If I had allowed myself to become discouraged, I never would have caught any of them," she said. "And I never would have met you."

"Scarlet," Clint said, "what if the fifth man is . . . gone? What if he's already died, either of natural causes or because someone else killed him?"

"This morning you said we had to assume that Wade was still heading for his brother, because it was the only course of action that made sense."

"That's right," he said. "I did say that."

"Well, the same thing applies here," she said. "I have to believe that the fifth man is still alive. I have to believe that I will have the chance to kill him. It's the only course of action that makes any sense to me."

Clint opened his mouth to reply, but then realized that there was no way he could argue her point. If she felt that strongly about it, it was the only thing that would keep her going.

But how long, he wondered, could vengeance drive her without having some sort of adverse effect on her?

Wade Grafton poured the remnants of his coffee into the fire, and then kicked dirt on it to finish the job. He gathered up his gear, stowed it in his saddlebags, and then saddled his horse. It took him a couple of tries to get the saddle on the animal's back, because of his wound, but he finally did it and cinched it up tight.

Before trying to mount he took a few moments to rest. Saddling the animal had winded him.

Leaning against his horse, he wondered again how he was going to tell Lee about what happened to Sam and Harley—and how he would explain that he hadn't killed the woman who'd killed them.

The woman, Scarlet, was an unusual woman—and she was in a business that was unusual for women . . . bounty hunter. She shouldn't be too hard to find, and he knew that Lee was going to want to find her.

He wanted to find her too, but not until he was fully recovered from his wound, and not until he had Lee and whatever men Lee had collected to back him up.

He had seen a lot of moves in his time, but she had gotten her gun out faster than anyone—any *man* he'd ever seen before—and that included his brother Lee.

Wade Grafton admitted to himself that Scarlet scared the shit out of him. He would, however, need something else to tell his brother.

TEN

It was hardly more than a shack, and it was in the middle of nowhere.

"What do you think?" Scarlet asked.

"There's a lean-to off to the right. Let's take a look at it."

They left their horses and approached the lean-to on foot. Under the roof of the lean-to they found one horse, an animal not much good for anything but pulling a rig. There was a beat-up rig behind the lean-to, but it looked as if it hadn't been used in some time.

"Nothing," Scarlet said, but Clint continued to look, and was rewarded.

In one corner of the lean-to he saw something, leaned over, and picked it up.

"What is it?" she asked.

"A shirt," he said, showing it to her.

"Blood," she said, "and a hole in the left shoulder. This was Grafton's."

"We'd better have a talk with the people inside."

"If there are any left alive," she said.

The woman's name was Ingrid Meek. She appeared to be about fifty, although Clint felt she was probably five or six years younger than that. She had obviously led a hard life.

Her body was all bone—high, sharp cheekbones, bony shoulders and hips which were not at all hidden by the threadbare dress she was wearing.

They told her they were looking for a man, and described Wade Grafton.

"Ain't seen 'im," she said.

"Are you alone?" Scarlet asked.

"Have been for years."

"Miss Meek," Clint said, taking the shirt out from behind his back, "we found this shirt in your lean-to."

She looked at the shirt in his hand and said, "It's an old shirt."

"This bloodstain is not yet a week old," Clint said.

"I can't help you," she said. "That's an old shirt of mine."

"Can't help us," Scarlet said, "or won't?"

"Don't make much of a difference," Ingrid Meek said.

"Are you afraid of something?" Clint asked.

She almost grinned. "I ain't afraid of nothin', mister. I just can't help you."

"You don't need a doctor, do you?"

"Doctor?"

"Well, if this is your shirt, you must have been hurt pretty bad."

"I do my own doctorin'," she said. "Have for years."

"I see," Clint said. "Well, thanks, anyway."

"Clint—" Scarlet started, but he cut her off.

"We'll be going."

Ingrid Meek nodded, backed into her shack, and closed the door.

"Why didn't you press her?" Scarlet asked as they walked back to their horses.

"No need to," he said. "This shirt is obviously not hers, and she obviously hasn't sustained this kind of a wound lately."

"So she was lying."

"Yes," Clint said, "but there was one thing I think she was telling the truth about."

"What's that?"

"That she does her own doctoring," he said. "I think she patched Grafton up, maybe let him rest a couple of days, and then he left."

"That would mean he's only a day or two ahead of us," Scarlet said.

"Right."

"But why wouldn't she tell us?"

"Who knows?" Clint said as they reached their horses. "Maybe they became friends."

"Maybe she is afraid," Scarlet said, mounting up.

"No," Clint said, climbing aboard Duke, "that's something else I think she was telling the truth about. I don't think there's much that would scare that lady."

"She must be awful lonely, living out here by herself," Scarlet said.

Clint stared at her for a few moments. "You may have hit it right there."

"Hit what?"

"She's lonely, and for a while she had a man in her life."

"You mean . . . her and Wade Grafton?"

"Odder things have happened," Clint said. "Just imagine a woman without a man for years, and then one falls right in her lap."

Scarlet frowned, looking back at the shack.

"I can't imagine her and Wade Grafton . . ."

"Neither can I," Clint said, "but let's not dwell on it. The border is a day ahead of us."

They wheeled their horses around and rode off.

Wade Grafton camped on the Texas side of the river, figuring to cross in the morning. The river was deep there, and the crossing might be treacherous. He'd need to rest himself for it.

He prepared some coffee and had some beef jerky with it. His shoulder was throbbing, but he tried to ignore it. Whoever the woman was, she'd turned out to be a pretty good doctor. She had probably kept him from bleeding to death, or dying from an infection. He supposed that was the reason he'd left her alive. Still, it had probably been a foolish move. He knew he'd wounded the red-haired bounty hunter, but she'd be on his trail soon enough. Might even come upon the shack and the woman. Would the woman keep her mouth shut about him, or would she give him away?

The fact that he was asking himself those questions told him that he'd made a mistake leaving her alive.

Well, he just wouldn't mention that to Lee. His brother was going to be angry enough at him without adding fuel to the fire.

Lee wouldn't stay mad at him forever, though. After all, the two of them were going to have to avenge the deaths of their brothers together, weren't they?

He finished his coffee and lay down with his blanket. He tried lying on his side, but his shoulder wouldn't allow it, so he turned onto his back and stared up at the stairs. He probably should have stayed alert, but the red-haired woman, Scarlet, was at least three or four days behind him—if she was that close—and he was too damned tired to stay awake, anyway. He needed a few decent meals to get his strength back, but he was still a couple of days away from that.

He hoped he had enough strength to make it to Domingo.

ELEVEN

As Wade had suspected, the crossing was not easy. To assure that he didn't fall off his horse in his weakened state, he tied his feet to the stirrups. He knew he was taking a chance on drowning if the horse went down, but he'd been riding this steeldust for four years now, and had confidence in him. That is, he had more confidence in the animal's chances of making the crossing than he did in his own ability to stay in the saddle.

Poised to enter the water, he took a deep breath and then urged the horse on.

"We're a day from the Rio Grande," Clint said as they broke camp that morning. "We can be there by nightfall."

"Can we cross at night?"

"That depends on how deep the water is and how strong the current is at the point we choose to make our crossing," he explained.

Scarlet finished kicking the fire to death and collected the utensils. They were traveling light, with no pack animals. Soon they would have to make a stop for supplies, but they figured Wade Grafton would be in at least the same position, and maybe worse.

They saddled their horses and mounted up and started the day's ride.

"Clint?"

"Yeah?"

"I want to talk."

Clint looked at her and asked, "Are you sure?"

She hesitated a moment, then nodded her head shortly and said, "I think so."

"Then I'm ready to listen," he said, "if that's all you want me to do."

"I don't know what I want you to do," she said, "but I'll talk and just jump in if you have a mind to."

"All right."

She fell silent then, and he was just beginning to think that she had changed her mind when she finally started speaking.

"To begin with," she said, "my real name is Alicia. Alicia Bogart."

"Alicia," Clint repeated. "I have a question already."

That brought a grin to her face and she said, "What is it?"

"From now on do I call you Alicia or Scarlet?"

"Scarlet," she answered, without hesitation. "Alicia's dead. She died when she was sixteen." Scarlet was sixteen the day she was raped and her family was killed. "I haven't even thought about her in the long time."

"What kind of girl was Alicia?"

"Like any other," Scarlet said. "Innocent, naive, worried about her first encounter with a boy . . ." She stopped and shook her head, as if trying to toss something off.

"Scarlet . . ."

"I'm all right," she said. "It's just . . . all coming back."

"Maybe you shouldn't talk about it just now," he suggested.

She bit her full underlip, then looked at him and said, "Maybe you're right. It's too damned painful to think about it, and there's no good reason to. It doesn't strengthen my resolve, because that's already like iron. All it does is make me cry, which makes me feel weak."

"Well," Clint said, "I can tell you from experience that you are not a weak woman. Not by a long sight."

"Thanks."

She hadn't said much, but she had told him her real name. Maybe, he hoped, she had started to make progress towards a time when she could put all the pain and vengeance behind her and live a normal life.

But what was a normal life for the woman called Scarlet? What was a normal life for a man like Clint Adams, whom others called The Gunsmith? They had both made their way with a gun for a long time—much longer for him than her—and he had already tried to find a normal life several times. He'd always ended up with a gun back in his hand, until he'd finally accepted the fact that he *was* living a normal life—normal for him.

Maybe Scarlet hadn't reached that point in her life, yet. At least, he hoped for her sake that she hadn't.

The crossing was as Wade Grafton had anticipated. When he and his horse got to the other side they were both exhausted.

On the other side he leaned over and untied both of his feet from the stirrups. That done, he started to get off the horse and ended up sliding off it to the ground. Hitting the ground jarred his injured shoulder, and he cried out and remained there on his back for a few moments, waiting for the pain to subside and catching his wind.

Suddenly, he became aware that he was not alone. He pushed himself up on his good elbow and looked around. About ten yards away were three mounted Mexicans, staring down at him.

"What are you lookin' at?" he demanded.

"It looks to me like a wet gringo," one of the Mexicans said, and the other two laughed.

They were of a kind, all mustachioed and dark-skinned, with bandoliers across their chests. They all seemed fairly amused at the wet gringo. That would work in Wade's favor. It gave him an edge if they didn't take him very seriously.

Wade pushed himself to a seated position, facing the three Mexicans. It was an extremely unthreatening position, which was the very reason he assumed it.

"Can I do something for you gents?" Wade asked.

"*Sí*, you can do something for us, gringo," the spokesman said. "You see, we are the toll collectors. When you cross the border in Mexico, you must pay the toll."

"And if I don't?"

The man shrugged and said, "If you do not pay, then you go no further—and you do not go back. *Comprende?*"

"Oh, I *comprende*," Wade said. "And how much is this toll?"

The man laughed, as did his companions. "That depends, gringo, on how much you have."

Wade held his good hand out to them and said, "I'm gonna get up. Don't get nervous."

"That is excellent advice for all of us, gringo," the man said. "Do not get nervous, and we will all live to see another day, eh?"

Wade doubted that these three men had any intention of letting him see another day.

"Yeah," Wade said to himself, standing up, keeping his body turned away from them so that his gun hand was not in their view. "Don't get nervous . . . get dead!"

It was a good test for his injured shoulder. He drew his gun, and had taken one of the Mexicans from his saddle before the other two even knew what was happening. As they fought to control their mounts he shot both of them. Their horses ran off, leaving all three men lying in the dirt.

Wade kept his gun out as he approached them. Two of them were clearly dead, as he had shot them in the head. The third man was seriously wounded in the chest, but still alive. He was the spokesman.

Wade approached him, kicked the man's weapon away, and stood and looked down at him as blood spurted from the man's chest.

"*Señor*," the man said, blood flowing from his mouth, "you are a tricky . . ."

Wade didn't find out what he was, because the man died in mid-sentence.

"Yeah," Wade said, ejecting the spent shells from his gun and replacing them with live rounds, "I'm tricky . . . and I'm back."

TWELVE

That night Clint and Scarlet camped on the Texas side of the border.

"It doesn't look too bad," Clint had said when they arrived, "but let's cross in the morning."

"Why not now?"

"When we get to the other side we'll have to be alert for border bandits," Clint said. "I'd rather deal with them in the morning than in the dark."

"All right."

Clint took care of the horses while Scarlet put on a pot of coffee and fried up some bacon and beans.

"Shall we set a watch for the night?" Scarlet asked while they ate.

"We could, but I don't think it's necessary," Clint said.

"What about the border bandits?"

"The *bandidos* work the other side of the border, not this side," Clint said. "They'll watch our fire and wait for us to cross."

"If they're there."

"That's right," Clint said, "if they're there."

"How do we know if they're there?"

"We'll find out tomorrow when we cross."

"How many will there be?"

"Who knows?"

"Aren't you worried?"

"Sure, I'm worried," Clint said. "But it's just something that we're going to have to deal with tomorrow. Either that, or we can turn back."

"No, we're not turning back. The Graftons are in Mexico. I'm sure of it."

"You won't be able to collect the bounty in Mexico," Clint pointed out.

"Then I'll just have to bring them back over the border," she said. "I'll collect at the nearest town."

"Fine."

"Will you be with me that long?"

"Scarlet," Clint said, "I'll be with you for as long as you need me."

"I'm not used to needing anyone, Clint."

"I know," Clint said. "I know that."

She hesitated, then said, "I'm afraid that if I let myself start needing you, I won't be able to stop."

"Everybody needs somebody sometime, Scarlet," Clint said, "but not all the time. All I can tell you is that I'm here when you need me, and I'll be gone when you don't. I can't promise you anything more than that."

She stared at him and said, "That's enough, Clint. That's more than enough."

THIRTEEN

The next morning Clint and Scarlet crossed the river with no trouble. It wasn't particularly deep, and there was no current to speak of. The only problem they might have had was border bandits, and as they reached the Mexican side, none materialized.

"Where to now?" Scarlet asked.

"Well, we can keep riding south and try to pick up a trail. . . ."

"Or?"

"Well, we didn't encounter any border bandits, but that doesn't mean that Wade Grafton was as lucky."

"Meaning what?"

"Meaning we could ride up and down the border here, a few miles each way, and just see if he's not lying dead somewhere."

"And if he's dead?"

"Then there'd be no point in going any further."

"Not for you, maybe."

"Scarlet—"

"Clint, Lee Grafton has pulled some big jobs over the past few years. If he's down here, and he's planning something, he'll be looking for men."

69

"And you expect to catch wind of it?"

"He'll be looking for men and guns," she said. "The word would have to be getting around."

Clint stared at her for a few moments, then said, "Let's cross that bridge when we come to it. Let's scout the border for a while and see what we find. We might fall a little further behind him, but if we find him we'll know something we didn't know before."

"All right," she agreed, but her jaw was set so sternly that he knew if they did or didn't find Wade Grafton's body, she was dead set on going on.

It was noon when Wade Grafton spotted the town of Domingo. It was still a ways off, but the ground was so flat that he could see the town ahead.

Because he didn't realize he was so close to Domingo he had stopped at a little town a few hours earlier to get some supplies. The place was so small it didn't even have a name, but it had a general store, and he'd picked up some supplies. Now he realized he needn't have bothered. What little food he'd eaten on the trail had not increased his strength. What he needed was some hot food and a bed for a few hours in Domingo, and then he'd be fine.

Maybe Lee would even let him eat and sleep before he made him explain what had happened to Harley and Sam.

He hoped so.

It was a little before noon, and they were looking down at the three bodies. Scarlet continued to stare at them while Clint walked around the area, checking out the ground.

"Bandits?" she said.

He nodded, still examining the ground.

"I guess they ran into a few gringos who weren't willing to be robbed," she said.

"One man."

"What?"

He was hunkered down on his heels, and now he stood up and walked to her.

"One man. He came up out of the water. Looks like he fell off his horse."

"Or maybe was shot off?"

"I don't think so," Clint said. "He was still healthy enough to do these three in. No, I think he fell off, which would indicate that if it's Grafton he wasn't quite strong enough to make the crossing here without it taking a toll. The water's deeper here than where we crossed, and the current's strong."

"So you're saying that Grafton killed these three?" she asked.

"I'm saying one man killed them," Clint said.

"He couldn't sit his horse, but he was well enough to outshoot these three?"

"Why not? They're just bandits, not hired guns. If he got the drop on them, two of them were probably dead before the third one knew what was going on."

"Is he good enough to have done that?"

"You tell me," Clint said. "You faced him."

She hesitated a moment, then said, "Well, he put a bullet in me, so I guess he's pretty good."

"Now we have another question."

"What's that?"

"We have a trail," he said. "Do we assume it's Grafton's and follow it?"

"Do we have a choice?" she asked. "There's not much else we can do."

"All right, then," he said. "Let's get to following it and see where it leads us."

When Lee Grafton wasn't in his room with Juanita, he was in the cantina where he'd found her. Not only had he taken over Juanita, but he'd also taken over the cantina. None of the townspeople even tried to get inside anymore, and the owner served Grafton with a smile affixed to his face. His eyes, however, remained frightened.

Grafton was working on a bottle of tequila when Sean Rock entered the cantina.

"You looking for me, Rock?"

Rock turned at the sound of Grafton's voice and saw him sitting at a corner table. Every time Rock found Grafton in the cantina, the man was seated at a different table.

"There's a rider coming across the flats towards town, Lee," Rock said.

Grafton looked at Rock sharply. "One rider?"

"Only one, riding slow."

"Do you know who it is?"

"Not yet," Rock said. "He's still too far away to recognize."

Grafton gripped the tequila bottle tightly, tilted it, and filled his glass.

"Let me know when you do recognize him."

"I've got Kerns and Cartwright on the roof."

"I want you on the roof, Rock," Grafton said. "I want you to let me know when *you* recognize him. Understand?"

"I understand, Lee."

"Get to it."

"Right."

Instead of leaving the cantina, Sean Rock took the stairs to the second floor. From there he made his way to the roof.

Grafton didn't like hearing that there was a lone rider approaching Domingo. He was waiting for his *three* brothers, not just one man. One man approaching could just have been a stranger, a drifter, but Grafton decided that this man was going to have to pay the price for not being his brothers.

Whoever the man was, he'd be sorry when he finally reached Domingo.

He'd find that he'd drifted into the wrong town.

For a moment, Wade Grafton thought that the town ahead of him was a mirage. The buildings were shimmering, but he told himself that was just because of the heat that was rising up from the ground. The buildings shimmered, but they never disappeared.

Once he felt himself slipping from his horse, and righted himself quickly. He didn't want to fall off because he might not get on again.

Sean Rock watched as the man got closer and closer to Domingo. Stupid damned name for a town, Domingo. Somebody had told him that it meant "Sunday," but that only made him more certain that it was a stupid name—a stupid name for a nothing town that he was getting pretty damn tired of. If he hadn't been with Lee Grafton for three years he might be grousing like some of the other men were. There were two or three men in town who had ridden with Grafton before, but there were many times that number who had never ridden with him. They had heard of him, though, both before they had gotten to town and since, and they were all still here. Grafton had been right about that. Nobody was about to run out on their piece of one of Grafton's pies just because they were getting impatient.

Rock squinted as the man came closer, thinking that he recognized him. Aside from Grafton, Kerns, and Cartwright, Rock was the only other man who knew all of the Grafton brothers on sight, and damned if this lone rider didn't look a helluva a lot like . . . like Wade Grafton.

But if Wade was riding in alone, where were Sam and Harley? And why did Wade look like he was about to fall off his animal?

Just as Rock was asking himself that question, the man did fall off his horse. Rock cursed. The only way to find out for sure who the man was, was to go out there and take a look.

He went downstairs to tell Lee what he thought, and did not relish bringing him the news.

He just hoped that Grafton would remember that Sean Rock had been with him for three years, and wouldn't take his anger out on him.

FOURTEEN

When Wade Grafton woke up he thought for a moment that he was still in that shack. He half expected the woman to come into the room, disrobe, and climb on top of him again—or was that a dream?

He looked around without moving his head and realized that he was in a different room, and in a different bed. When the door opened a woman did walk in, but this one was different.

Was she ever.

This woman was Mexican, with dark skin, long dark hair, and big, pear-shaped breasts barely confined by a low-cut peasant blouse.

Behind her came his brother, Lee.

"Wade?" Lee said.

"Lee?"

"How are you feeling?"

Wade frowned. How was he feeling? The last thing he remembered was falling from his horse.

"I fell off my horse."

"Sean Rock rode out and picked you up," Lee said. "He brought you into town. Juanita here rewrapped your shoulder."

"Thank you, Juanita," Wade said.

The woman did not answer.

"She didn't do it for you," Lee said. "She did it because I told her to."

"Oh."

"Juanita," Lee said, "go and get my brother and me a bottle of whiskey."

"And some food," Wade said.

"Food," Lee said to her.

"*Sí*," she said.

"Hot food," Wade said as she left the room. He hoped she had heard him.

Lee walked to the window, picked up a wooden chair, brought it back to the bed, and sat down.

"You sure you're feeling all right?" Lee asked.

"Sure, Lee," Wade said. "I'm okay."

"Can you talk?"

"Sure."

"Good," Lee said. "What the fuck happened, Wade? Where are Sam and Harley?"

Wade swallowed hard, then tried to moisten his mouth before he spoke. He wished they already had that bottle of whiskey.

"They're dead, Lee."

He watched Lee's face, which did not betray any emotion whatsoever. He waited a while, to see what his brother was going to say.

"All right," Lee finally said, "let me have all of it, Wade."

Wade started talking, wondering how he could tell it without having himself come out badly.

Clint and Scarlet rode into a town that was so small it didn't seem to have a name. Actually, it looked like it used to be a town, but so many of the buildings were damaged and vacant that it could hardly be called that anymore.

As they reached the center of the street they found there were more buildings there which were still in one piece and inhabited. This included a cantina and a general store.

"Let's get some food in our bellies, and ask some questions," Clint said.

They stopped their horses in front of the cantina, dismounted, and went inside.

"*Buenos días, señor y señorita,*" the bartender called out. He was an immensely fat man who looked as if he could not have come out from behind the bar if he tried. "And what can I get for you?"

"Do you have hot food?"

"*Sí,*" the man said, "*tortillas, enchiladas, a ros con pollo—*"

"Bring it all," Clint said, "and some beer."

"*Sí,*" the man said again, "*cerveza.* Angelina!" he shouted.

From a doorway near the bar came a girl. She appeared to be eighteen or nineteen. She had long dark hair, big hoop earrings, and pert breasts under a lace blouse.

"*Si, Papa?*"

The man relayed the order to her in rapid-fire Spanish. The girl looked around to see who had ordered all that food, and when her eyes fell on Clint they widened.

"*Sí, Papa,*" she said, and went inside to get the food.

The bartender proved he could indeed come out from behind the bar when he did so to bring them two cold beers.

"*Cerveza,*" he said. "*Mucho frío, señor.* Very cold."

"Good," Clint said. "*Gracias.*"

"*Por nada, señor,*" the man replied. "My daughter will bring the food soon."

"Do you speak Spanish?" Scarlet said, after a couple of healthy swallows of beer to cut the dust.

"You just heard most of it."

"I wonder how they make a living here."

"The same way they are now, I guess," Clint said. "Feeding hungry strangers who pass through."

"If that's the case," Scarlet said, "the prices must be high."

Clint inhaled the aroma coming from the kitchen and said, "Smells to me like it might be worth it."

"We'll see," Scarlet said.

Soon enough Angelina appeared, bearing a huge tray that seemed impossibly big and too laden for her to carry. Still, she made it across the floor to their table without dropping a thing, and laid everything out on the table. That done, she put the tray down on a nearby table and stood by their table, her hands held behind her back, her chest pushed out for Clint's benefit. He could see the outline of her large nipples against the fabric of her blouse.

"Can I get you anything else, *señor*?" she asked, hopefully.

"I think we have plenty here, Angelina," Clint said. "*Gracias.*"

"*De nada,*" she said, with a small curtsy. She collected her empty tray and walked back to the kitchen. Before reentering, however, she turned and gave Clint another long—and longing—look.

"I don't think she was referring to food," Scarlet said to Clint.

"Scarlet," he scolded her, "she's just a child."

"Hardly a child," Scarlet said, "and I noticed the way you were looking at her chest."

"I couldn't help it," he said. "She was pushing it all the way out."

Scarlet laughed and said, "I thought she was going to hurt her back."

They both laughed, and fell to eating. As it turned out, the food was worth the wait and, they agreed, would be worth almost any price.

After the time they'd spent on the trail, eating beans and bacon, it was a pleasure to have some real food again.

FIFTEEN

By the time Juanita returned with a bottle of whiskey and some food, Wade had told his story and was waiting for Lee's reaction.

Juanita laid the tray on a table by the bed, and turned to present Lee with the bottle of whiskey. He stood up, took it from her, and then backhanded her across the face.

"Go and wait for me in the room," he told her.

As she left the room, walking proudly, shoulders back and chin held high, even though she wanted to flee, Lee opened the bottle and took several long swallows.

"What the hell did you hit her for?" Wade asked.

Lee took the bottle away from his mouth and said to his brother, "Because I can't hit you while you're laid up, you sonofabitch!"

"Aw, Lee—"

"Shut up, Wade!" Lee said. "How could you let some woman kill them and live?"

"I told you, Lee," Wade said, "she weren't just any woman."

"Yeah, you told me," Lee said, disgustedly waving his brother to be quiet. He hesitated a moment, then handed the bottle of whiskey to his brother. "Drink some of that and have something to eat. After that, get some rest. I'll be back later."

"Lee, listen—"

Lee held up his hand to silence his older brother.

"We'll talk about it later, Wade," Lee said. "I've got to decide how this is going to affect the job I've got planned."

"Lee—"

"Later," Lee said, remarkably calm now. "Later, Wade. Get some rest."

As Lee left the room Wade stared after him, then tilted the bottle up and drained half of it.

That hadn't been half as bad as he'd thought it was going to be.

Lee Grafton went back to his own room, where Juanita was waiting. She was seated on the bed, still fully dressed. There was a trickle of blood from the left corner of her mouth, and her long, black hair was in a state of disarray. She had never looked sexier, but for the first time since meeting her, she was failing to arouse him. He had too much on his mind, thanks to his brother Wade.

His last living brother . . .

"Juanita," he said, "go and get me a bottle of whiskey."

Happy to get away from him, Juanita got off the bed, put on her shoes, and left the room.

Lee Grafton wondered when she'd get tired of his treatment and try to stick a knife in him.

SIXTEEN

After they finished their meal Angelina rushed out to clean the table, as if she had been watching them. Scarlet noticed that the Mexican girl had tugged her blouse down a few inches, until the brown circles of her nipples almost showed. Not without some amusement she watched Clint to see what his reaction would be.

"Would you like some coffee?" Angelina asked Clint. She was ignoring Scarlet.

"Yes, I would," Clint said, "and I think my companion would too."

"Companion?" Angelina said, looking at Scarlet with a puzzled frown. "Does that mean that she is not your woman?"

"That's what it means, yes," Scarlet said.

"He is not your man?"

Scarlet looked at Clint, then at Angelina, and said, "No, he is not."

"Do you have a woman?" Angelina asked him.

"No, Angelina, I don't."

That made Angelina smile—a smile so big it made her face shine.

"I will be your woman," she said.

Scarlet watched Clint, interested in his response.

"That's very nice, Angelina," Clint said, "and you're very beautiful, but I will be leaving within the hour."

"So soon?" Angelina asked, looking sad.

"Yes."

"Perhaps you would like to . . . be with me before you leave?"

Scarlet fought to hide a smile.

"I wish I had the time," Clint said, "but I only have time for a cup of coffee, and then I must be going."

She looked ever sadder for a moment, then her face brightened.

"Perhaps you will pass this way again?"

"Perhaps I will."

"And stay longer?"

"If I come this way again," he said, "I will definitely stay longer."

That made her happy. "I will go and get the coffee."

"*Gracias*," he said.

When Angelina had gone back to the kitchen Clint looked at Scarlet, and caught her looking at him.

"What?" he said.

"You handled that very well."

"Thank you."

"I notice you handle most women very well," she said, "no matter what age they are."

"It's a knack," he said modestly.

"Too bad we only have time for a cup of coffee," she said.

"Why?"

"Well . . . we could put up for the night, and you could show me your knack."

He smiled and said, "We can do that on the trail, in a bedroll."

"Yes," she said, "I suppose we can."

When they finished eating they walked over to the general store to pick up some supplies. They also asked some questions. The clerk there, who was also the owner, remembered Wade Grafton when they described him.

"*Sí, senor*," the store owner said, "there was such a man as you have described. He walked so"—he turned his shoulder in a bit—"as if he were hurt or . . . or wounded."

"He was," Clint said. "He is also a dangerous Americano who might kill some Mexican citizens while he is here if we don't stop him."

"And you?" the man asked. "You are not a dangerous Americano?"

"Only to him," Clint said. "Did he say where he was going?"

"No, I am sorry," the clerk said. "He did not say anything, except to order his supplies."

"Did you happen to see which way he went when he left town?"

"I did not leave the store to watch him," the man said, shaking his head. "I am sorry, but I can only tell you that he was here."

"That's enough," Clint said to the man. "That's more than enough."

He put more money on the counter than they owed for the supplies, and then picked up the supplies. "Thank you."

"*Por nada, señor*."

Clint and Scarlet left the store and stopped just outside
to stow the supplies away in their saddlebags. Scarlet had
not spoken a word inside.

"Well," she said now, "at least we know that he came
this way."

"It's more than we've known for sure since we started,"
Clint said. "We'll keep heading south, and maybe we'll
bump into him."

"Maybe we will."

SEVENTEEN

Making love on the ground had its advantages, and its disadvantages.

One advantage was that, with no yield beneath them, it made for maximum penetration.

Scarlet was finding that out now. With no give beneath him as she came down on Clint, it felt as if his penis were driving up inside of her, between her breasts. She caught her breath every time she came down on him, and when her time came she ground herself down on him as he exploded inside of her.

One disadvantage was how your back felt afterward.

"Are you all right?" she asked, laughing.

"Just a bit of back pain," he said, sitting up. "It'll pass."

She got around behind him, still naked, and began to rub his back. "How's that?"

"Much better."

She continued to rub his back, pressing hard, and then leaned into him, pressing her breasts to his back.

"Ooh," he said, "that feels even better."

He turned and took her into his arms, drawing her into his lap. He kissed her hard and long, and then looked at her body, with the firelight dancing off of it.

"God, you're beautiful."

"How have you been able to keep your hands off me since we left Ralston?" she asked.

She slid from his lap and started to dress.

"I guess I didn't think you wanted me to. . . ."

"I didn't," she said.

He grabbed his shirt and put it on. "Why not?"

"I don't know," she said, pulling her pants on. "I suppose I don't think I should have that much . . . pleasure."

"Until you've finished what you have to do?"

She looked at him, and nodded.

When they were both dressed she poured them each a cup of coffee from the pot on the fire. He strapped on his gun and crouched by the fire. She left her gunbelt draped over her shoulder.

"We're in Mexico now, so we'd better set a watch," he said.

"Four hours each?" she asked.

"Fine," he said, "I'll take the first."

She seemed poised to argue, but she didn't. "All right."

They had made love on his bedroll, so she turned hers down.

"In the future," he said, "we'd better save the good stuff for hotels."

She looked at him over her shoulder.

"It's too dangerous to be that . . . preoccupied out here."

She nodded, and said, "I agree."

He watched her settle down on her bedroll, her back to him and the fire, and then looked up at the sky. He could still taste her on his lips, and smell her.

It wouldn't be easy, keeping his hands off her the rest of the way.

The next morning Lee Grafton woke and looked over at Juanita, sleeping next to him. He reached over and pulled the sheet off her without waking her. He looked at the curve of her naked back, the swell of her firm, rounded buttocks. She was a big woman, full in the breasts and thighs without being fat. He liked that. He enjoyed the way she felt beneath him when he was ramming himself into her, and she was arching her back to meet his thrusts. Even though she didn't like him, he knew she enjoyed the sex as much as he did. If he was nice to her, he felt she would have fallen in love with him.

He didn't want that.

Abruptly, he lifted his hand and brought it down on the right buttock, hard. She screamed and came awake, reaching back to rub away the sting.

"Go and get my breakfast ready," he said. "I'll be down in half an hour."

"Oh . . ." she said burying her face in the pillow.

He lifted his hand and slapped her on the other buttock—not as hard, but it still stung her into action. Wordlessly, she got out of bed and dressed. He watched her with pleasure, the way her breasts hung down and slapped gently together while she pulled on her skirt. The way they lifted and jutted when she put her hands over her head and put on her blouse. The way they pressed together, confined now by the blouse, as she put on her shoes.

"What would you like?" she asked.

"Eggs," he said, "with none of that hot sauce you put on them."

"And?"

"Spuds."

She made a face, but turned and left the room to have his breakfast prepared.

"And biscuits!" he called after her.

After she had gone Lee dressed and walked down the hall to the room he'd had his brother Wade taken to. As he entered he saw that his brother was awake.

"How do you feel?"

"Stronger," Wade said. "Strong enough to get out of this bed and have some breakfast."

"All right," Lee said. "Get up and get dressed. Meet me downstairs in fifteen minutes."

Wade threw back the sheet and swung his feet around to the floor. "I'll be there."

When Scarlet woke him he smelled the coffee and the bacon.

"Come on, sleepyhead," she said. "We have time for a quick breakfast."

"You're in a hurry today," he said, coming instantly awake.

"I have a feeling," she said, brightly. She went to the fire to spoon out the breakfast.

"What kind of a feeling?"

"I think," she said, handing him a plate of bacon, "that we are going to find our man today."

He stared at her, somewhat amazed—or puzzled—at her bright mood. Could it be that her woman's intuition was at work here? Clint's life had been saved enough times by his own intuition, so he wasn't about to look down his nose at hers.

"If we find him," Clint said, "we're also going to find his brother, and his brother's men. You know that as well as I do."

"I only want the Grafton brothers," she said. "The other men are of no importance to me."

"No importance, perhaps, but of concern, that's for sure. It'll be kind of hard to get to them without going through the others," Clint said. "And as good as we are together, I doubt that we can go through them alone, just the two of us."

"Then we'll just have to go around them," she said, "won't we?"

"Maybe we'll have to make that decision when the right time comes," Clint said. "Once we've seen what we're up against."

"Clint," Scarlet said, "you don't have to do this, you know."

He smiled across the fire at her and said, "I know."

EIGHTEEN

When Wade Grafton came downstairs to meet his brother, breakfast was waiting for him. His brother was already halfway through his own.

"It smells good," Wade said, sitting down gingerly.

"How's your shoulder?" Lee asked.

"Fine," Wade said. "My back's a little stiff, though, from lyin' in bed so long. Jesus, a soft bed can make my back stiffer than sittin' a horse."

"You're getting old."

Wade gave his brother a quick look. "Is that what you think happened, Lee?" he asked. "I'm gettin' old? I lost my nerve?"

"Eat your breakfast and don't get your back up," Lee said.

"I did what I could, you know," Wade said. "She was too fast for us, too fast for the three of us."

"A woman?" Lee had to ask.

"Yes, a woman," Wade said.

"Women are for cooking, for cleaning, for bedding," Lee said. "I find it hard to accept that a woman outdrew three men, killing two of them and wounding a third—and they were my own brothers!"

"I was there!" Wade said stridently. There were no other diners in the room, or he certainly would have attracted attention. Lee Grafton would have no one else around him while he ate, not even his own men.

"Take it easy, Wade," Lee said. "There's just the two of us left, you know. We can't afford to start fighting each other."

"I just want you to know," Wade said, "I did what I could. I took a bullet, and I wounded her."

"You didn't tell me that before."

"Well, I did. I hit her."

"Bad?"

Wade frowned and said, "I don't think so. I think I got her in the arm."

"What else can you tell me about her?"

"They call her Scarlet," Wade said. "She's a bounty hunter, and she was on our trail for weeks, maybe even more."

Wade described the woman to his brother, who listened intently.

"Believe me," Wade said, "if she hadn't been after us, she was the kind of woman any of the three of us would have loved to take to bed."

"This doesn't figure," Lee said. "A beautiful woman working as a bounty hunter."

"Damn it," Wade said around a mouthful of eggs, "get that notion out of your head. This woman is dangerous— and she's probably on my trail!"

"If she is," Lee said, "then all we have to do is wait here for her."

"What about the job?"

"That can wait," Lee said. "We've got unfinished business first."

"What about your men?"

"They'll wait," Lee said.

"How long?"

"As long as I tell them to."

"You hired patient men?" Wade said in surprise.

"No," Lee said, "but they'll have to learn it."

Wade was going to say something else, but he saw Lee look beyond him. Moments later Sean Rock was standing beside their table.

"What?" Lee asked.

Rock looked at Wade and asked, "How're you feeling, Wade?"

"Stronger, Sean," Wade said. "Thanks for going out there after me."

Rock shrugged, and looked at Lee.

"Go on, Rock," Lee said, "tell me how impatient the men are."

"Everybody figures now that Wade is here we'll go ahead with the job."

"Everybody figures wrong," Lee said. "Harley and Sam were killed, and we're waiting right here until the killer finds us."

"How's he gonna do that?"

"She'll be along," Lee said. "She'll be trailing Wade here."

Rock laughed, and then frowned. "She?"

"That's right," Lee said. "A tall, red-haired gal, wearing a gun."

"She killed Harley and Sam?"

"And shot me," Wade said.

"Hey, wait—"

"Don't ask questions!" Lee said, harshly. "You know me. Would I kid about something like that?"

"Well . . . no, Lee, no, you wouldn't," Sean Rock stammered.

"Then tell Kerns and Cartwright to get back on the rooftops and watch for her."

"Will she be alone?"

Lee looked at Wade.

"I don't know," Wade said. "She didn't have anyone with her in Ralston."

Lee looked at Rock. "If she's smart, she'll have someone with her—a lot of someones . . . but we're dealing with a woman, after all."

"What's that mean?"

"That means be alert. Put some more men on the rooftops, in case she's not alone."

"Do you think she'll bring a posse?"

Lee rubbed his jaw. "All right," he said. "Send two men out a few miles from town. If they spot a posse, have one of them come back to warn us."

"All right."

Rock started to walk away and Lee stopped him.

"Rock, tell them that one man should return to town whether she's alone or has someone with her. We'll have to know what to expect."

"Right."

Lee looked at his brother, then looked down at the cold remains of his breakfast.

Wade had already finished his breakfast, even though he'd started after Lee.

"Are you gonna finish that?" he asked, indicating his brother's plate.

"What? No, go ahead."

Wade reached for his brother's plate, set it in front of him, and continued to eat.

"How can you eat that?"

"I want to be strong enough when she gets here," Wade said. "I want to be strong enough to kill her."

"Don't worry," Lee said, "we'll both do that."

"You know," Wade said, "I thought you'd be a lot madder at me."

Lee stared hard at his brother and said, "I am, Wade. I couldn't be angrier with you—but you're my last brother, aren't you?"

Wade looked back at Lee, into his cold eyes, and thought, Lucky for me I am.

NINETEEN

"Wait a minute."

Scarlet reined her horse in and looked over at Clint. "What is it?"

"We passed a sign a while back. It said that the next town was Domingo."

"So?"

Clint looked around, standing in his stirrups. "I've been here before—not exactly here, but in this area. It's flat."

"I can see that."

"Well, it's so flat that as we approach Domingo we'll be seen for miles."

"Yes?"

"That red hair of yours," he said, "it'll give us away for sure."

She looked up, as if she could see her hair. "I'll tuck it under."

"That won't do."

"Then what?"

"Stay here."

"What?"

"I'll ride into Domingo alone," he said. "I'll know

Wade Grafton when I see him, from your description. If he's there, I'll know."

"I can't let you go in there alone."

"You'll walk your horse in after dark, Scarlet," he said. "When you get there, I'll be waiting. If the Graftons aren't there, then we'll just move on."

"And if they are?"

Clint stared at her and then said, "Then we'll have some very serious thinking to do, won't we?"

She poked him in the chest with her forefinger and said, "Just make sure you don't get killed before I get there."

"I'll try my best."

Scarlet watched Clint ride off, and then looked around her.

"What the hell am I going to do out here all day?" she asked herself, helplessly.

As Clint came within sight of the town of Domingo he knew Lee Grafton would have some lookouts posted. He deliberately rode at a loping pace, as if he didn't have a care in the world.

Nothing could have been further from the truth.

"Rider coming," Sean Rock said to Ted Kerns. "I'll go down and tell Lee and Wade."

"Lee *and* Wade? I thought you were second in command," Kerns said.

"You know better than that, Ted," Rock said.

They both looked out at the rider again.

"Know him?" Kerns asked.

"Naw," Rock said. "You?"

"No," Kerns said, squinting. "He ain't in no particular hurry, is he?"

"No, he ain't," Rock said. "He should be here in about fifteen minutes, though. We'd better get ready for him."

"He don't have red hair."

"But he's wearing a gun," Rock said.

He walked to the end of the roof and waved to Cartwright, on a roof across the street with a man named Wilde. He pointed to the rider, and Cartwright nodded. If the man hadn't seen the rider already, he was aware of him now.

"I'm going downstairs, Ted," Rock said. "Keep watching him."

"I'll keep watching him," Kerns said to himself after Rock had left, "but how much harm can one man do?"

TWENTY

As Clint reached the edge of Domingo, where its main street started, he saw the men on the rooftops, watching him. There were three of them, one to his left, and two to his right. They were all holding rifles, and although they were not pointing at him, they were held at the ready.

He passed them, but could still feel them watching his back. Ahead of him several men had stepped out into the street. He only recognized one of them.

Wade Grafton.

He could tell it was Grafton from Scarlet's description, and from the way the man was standing, favoring his injured shoulder.

Clint continued to ride, and the men slowly moved out into the center of the street, blocking his path. When he reached them, he halted Duke's progress and looked down at the three men. The center man strongly resembled Wade Grafton, and that plus the fact that the other men seemed to defer to him, even by their posture, made him Lee Grafton.

"One of you fellas Lee Grafton?" he asked.

The man in the center said, "I'm Lee Grafton. What can I do for you?"

"I heard you were looking for men for a big job."

Lee Grafton folded his arms across his chest and frowned up at Clint.

"Where did you hear that?"

Clint looked down at each man's face in turn. They all had the same expression on their faces—skepticism.

"Around."

"Around?"

"That's what I said," Clint said. "Around."

The posture he took in the saddle was one that he copied from many men he had known over the years, men who'd thought they were better than other men. He now returned the looks of skepticism with arrogance, and a touch of condescension, both of which he was stealing from the hardcases he had known in his life.

"You rode in here all alone to join us?" Lee Grafton asked.

Clint laughed shortly and said, "What was I supposed to do, bring my mother?"

"Why?"

"Why what?"

"Why do you want to join us?"

"I've heard of you," Clint said. "I heard you were smart, and tough, and fair, and that men who rode with you made out all right."

"And is that what you want to do?" Lee asked. "Make out all right?"

"I hope to make out better than all right."

"Uh-huh," Lee said. He still had his arms folded across his chest, but both Wade Grafton and the other man had their hands down by their sides, near their guns.

"What makes you think you're good enough to ride with me?"

"I heard you needed good men," Clint said. He looked around him, noticed that there were men on both sides of the street as well as on the roof, and in front of him. He gave Wade Grafton and the other man pointed looks, then turned back to Lee Grafton.

"I don't see that you have an overabundance of them right now."

"Hey, friend—" the third man said, but Lee Grafton cut him off.

"Easy, Rock," Lee said.

Clint could hear some of the other men grumbling at the remark as well.

"What's your name, friend?" Lee asked.

"West," he said, taking the last name of one of his best friends. "Rick West." He named himself after Jim West and Rick Hartman.

"Tell me something, Mr. West," Lee asked, "what can you do that these men can't do?"

"Well, for one thing," Clint said, "I can outshoot any man you have."

"You can make a statement like that without having seen any of my men shoot?"

"Yes."

"You're that sure of yourself?"

"Yes."

"Let me shoot against him, Lee," Rock said. "I'll show him—"

Lee waved Sean Rock into silence.

"This is Sean Rock," Lee said to Clint. "You want to shoot against him?"

"I'll shoot against any of your men," Clint said, "or all of them."

"I have twenty-three men."

"Twenty-four," Clint said.

"Counting yourself already?"

"No," Clint said, "I'm counting you."

Lee Grafton laughed. "Are you saying you can out-shoot me?"

"That's what I'm saying."

Lee looked at Wade and Rock in turn, an arrogant look of his own on his face. He looked really amused at Clint's contention.

"You know, West," Lee said, "you got a lot of *cojónes* coming in here and making statements like that."

"Why?" Clint said. "If I prove I can outshoot any of you, I'm of value to you. You're not going to let something like pride, or ego, rob you of the services of a good man when you've got a big job planned, are you?"

"Let me take him, Lee," Rock said. "I'll plant him in the ground."

"My man wants to face you in the street," Lee said. "Are you ready for that?"

"I'm ready, if that's what you want," Clint said, "but why cost yourself a good man?"

"You're not one of his men," Sean Rock said.

"I wasn't talking about me, friend."

Rock made a move to charge Clint, but Lee Grafton stopped him.

"All right, Mr. West," Lee said. "You'll get your chance."

"Now?"

Lee shook his head. "Not yet. My man Cunningham here will take care of your horse."

Clint stepped down and handed Duke's reins to Cunningham.

"That's a fine-looking animal you've got there, Rick," Lee Grafton said.

"Yeah," Sean Rock said to Clint, "I'll take him, after I kill you."

Clint ignored Rock, which he had already found was the best way to handle the man.

"What about my gear?" Clint asked. "Can you stow it somewhere?"

"Let's worry about your gear," Lee Grafton said, draping his arm over Clint's shoulders, "later."

TWENTY-ONE

Lee Grafton kept his arm draped over Clint's shoulders all the way into the cantina.

"Have a seat, Rick," Lee Grafton said. "Is it all right if I call you Rick?"

"Sure," Clint said, "for now."

"For now," Lee said, with a grin. "What are you drinking, Rick?"

"Beer," Clint said, "cold."

"Cold beer for my . . . friend," Lee said to the bartender.

"*Sí, señor*," the man said.

"See the bean-eater here, Rick?" Lee said, indicating the bartender. "We took over this town, oh, two weeks or so ago, and that's how long we've been drinking in this cantina. If I wanted this bean-eater dead, he'd be dead by now, don't you agree?"

"I suppose so."

"And yet look at his hands." The bartender was putting a beer mug on top of the bar, and his hands were shaking visibly.

"He's scared," Clint said.

"Bet your ass he's scared," Lee said, "and do you know what that makes him?"

Lee walked over to the table, carrying Clint's beer.

"Sure," Clint said. "It makes him a smart man."

Lee looked at Clint in surprise, because Clint had said what *he* was about to say.

"You're a smart man too, aren't you, Rick?"

"That's right," Clint said. He reached out and took the beer from Lee with a steady hand. "I am."

"Sure you are," Lee said, sitting opposite him. "That's why you want to hitch your wagon to my team. Isn't that so?"

Clint took a sip from the beer and set the mug down on the table. "Is this all part of the test, Grafton?"

"What test?"

"The test to see if I get to be one of your men," Clint said. "I mean, there's more to the test than just shooting, isn't there?"

"If you can shoot," Lee said, "there'll be more, yeah."

"Well, then, let's solve that question right now," Clint said. "Bartender?"

"*Sí, señor?*" the frightened bartender said.

"Set five shot glasses up on the bar, upside down."

The bartender nodded, and did as he was told.

"What's this gonna—" Sean Rock started to ask, but he didn't have a chance to finish.

The bartender had hardly removed his hand from the fifth glass when Clint drew from his seated position and fired five shots in quick succession. All five shot glasses shattered so quickly it looked as if they had just disappeared.

Clint ejected the five spent shells and swiftly replaced them with live rounds, then returned the gun to his holster.

Sean Rock's mouth was open, and Wade Grafton was

also gaping. To Lee Grafton's credit, he managed not to look impressed.

"That's impressive," Lee said, "very impressive. Fast, and accurate. Very good . . . but glasses don't shoot back, do they?"

"Well," Clint said, picking up his beer, "the only way you can test me further is to stand one of your men up in front of me and see if I shoot him down." Clint looked at Sean Rock and said, "Hey, Sean, you still want to shoot against me out in the street?"

Rock turned and looked at Clint, swallowed hard, and looked at Lee Grafton.

"If Lee says so," Rock said, without much conviction.

Lee actually looked like he was considering it, and then shook his head and said, "Naw, forget it, Sean." He looked at Clint and said, "Sean's been with me too long for me to let you kill him."

"Does that mean I'm in?"

Lee considered it.

"Well, you can shoot, you're smart, and you've got guts," Lee said. "You proved that just by riding in here."

"That could have been dumb."

"No," Lee said, "you're not dumb—you're a damn sight more than dumb."

"So?"

Lee looked at Wade, who had taken a seat at another table. "Wade?"

"We can use a man who can shoot like him, Lee," Wade said, giving his brother an extra long look that did not escape Clint.

"Sean."

Rock, thinking his boss was asking for his opinion,

started to speak, but Lee said, "Get me a beer," and Rock closed his mouth.

"Sure."

Rock got a beer from the bartender and carried it over to Lee. The look he gave Clint was no longer an arrogant one. There was even respect in it, but it was a hell of a long way from being a friendly look.

"You've got my brother's approval, Rick," Lee said. "That counts for a lot, but that doesn't mean you've got mine. I'm going to reserve that for a while. You can understand that, can't you?"

"I can understand that."

"I thought you would. Meanwhile," Lee said, raising his beer mug, "welcome to the club, Rick West."

"Thanks," Clint said, thinking that he was joining something that was certainly not a "club." "Or considering where we are, *gracias*."

They both drank until the mugs were empty, and then lowered them.

"Sean, why don't you take Rick over to the hotel and get him a room—a good room."

"Lee," Rock said, "all the rooms at the hotel are taken."

Lee turned his head slowly to look at Rock and said, "So put somebody out, Sean. I want Rick to be real comfortable. Understand?"

Rock stared at Lee for a moment, then looked at Clint and said, "I understand. Come on. I'll show you to your room."

Clint stood up and said to Lee, "Thanks for the beer."

He followed Sean Rock out of the cantina. He knew he had impressed the man, but he also knew that he had made a bad enemy out of him.

TWENTY-TWO

After "Rick West" and Sean Rock had left, Wade came over to sit with Lee.

"What do you think, Lee?" Wade asked.

"What do I think?" Lee repeated, looking off into space, pursing his lips thoughtfully. "I think that nobody shoots that well and manages to stay totally unknown, and I never heard of Mr. Rick West. I think I'm going to keep a close eye on him."

"You don't think that's his real name?"

"Let's just say I'm not all that ready to believe him just yet."

"Why keep him around, then?"

Lee ticked off the points on the fingers of his left hand. "Because he's smart, he's got guts, and we can use some of that combination around here. Also, he can shoot, can't he?"

"He can do that."

"Yeah," Lee said. "If he's who he says he is, he can be a valuable asset to us."

"How do we make sure he is who he says he is?" Wade asked.

"When that lady who's trailing you gets here," Lee said, "I think I'm going to have Ricky boy kill her for us. Kill two birds with one stone, you know?"

"I sort of wanted to do that myself," Wade said, frowning.

Lee looked Wade right in the eyes and said, "Well, now, you had your chance to do that, didn't you?"

That was when Wade knew that Lee wasn't going to forgive and forget all that easily.

Rock made Clint wait in the lobby of the two-story adobe hotel while he cleared a room for him. Clint didn't protest about putting someone out of their room because Rick West wouldn't do that. Rick West would expect this kind of treatment.

Rock returned to the lobby and said, "Okay, follow me, West."

They went upstairs and Rock showed Clint where his room was. It was small, with a bed and a dresser, and a pitcher and bowl for washing.

"Ain't much," Clint said.

"You got complaints?" Rock said. "Take them to Lee yourself."

"It'll do," Clint said, "for now."

"Yeah," Rock said, "I thought it might."

He started to leave, closing the door behind him, but stopped and stuck his head back into the room. "I just got one piece of advice for you, West."

"What's that, Rock?"

"Don't get in my way."

"I'll make a note."

"Yeah," Rock said, and left, pulling the door closed behind him.

Clint looked out the window, found that it overlooked an alley. He looked at the bed, which was unmade, and made a mental note to get himself some fresh sheets before going to sleep in it.

Juanita closed the door to the room she shared with Lee Grafton. She had been looking out the front window when Sean Rock and the newcomer had come out of the cantina. She had been watching the whole time, starting with the newcomer's arrival, and knew that the man had faced down both Grafton brothers and Sean Rock without getting killed.

That made him interesting.

And she had been watching, with her door opened just a sliver, when Rock had led the man down the hall, and she saw that the man was very good-looking.

That made him *very* interesting.

Scarlet hadn't started a fire. There wasn't all that much around for her to use to make one, and she'd decided not to build one until it was absolutely necessary.

She hadn't unsaddled her horse either. She wanted to be ready to move on a moment's notice.

She sat on the ground, staring off into the distance the way Clint had gone, and chewed on some dried beef.

She wasn't thinking about the Grafton brothers at that moment. It was her elusive "fifth man" that she was thinking about. Abruptly, she shook her head to dispel those thoughts. Not concentrating on the business at hand was a good way to get herself and Clint killed.

With Clint Adams going out of his way to help her, the last thing she wanted to do was get him killed.

You don't do that to the only friend you've got in the world.

• • •

When the knock sounded on the door Clint was puzzled. He didn't know anyone in town, and Rock had barely had time to get back to the saloon, let alone be sent back by Grafton—and if it was Rock, he certainly would have knocked a lot harder than that.

Clint walked to the door and opened it. The woman standing in the hall was wearing a peasant blouse much like the one young Angelina had been wearing, but where Angelina had had petite breasts, this woman had a pair of breasts like melons, and the peasant blouse was doing little in the way of concealing them.

"Well, hello," Clint said.

"I am Juanita," she said, in not too heavily accented English.

"I'm . . . Rick West."

"Rick?"

"That's right."

"You will be working for Lee Grafton now?"

"That's right," Clint said, "for a while, anyway."

"You are in Room Four."

Clint looked at the door and nodded. "That's right, Room Four."

"I am in *ocho*," she said, "eight, down the hall."

He looked down the hall and saw that the door to her room was open. "I see."

Clint waited for the woman to say something else, and was surprised when she simply turned, walked back down the hall, entered her room, and closed the door.

Frowning, he stepped back into his room and closed the door.

TWENTY-THREE

"Did you put him to bed?" Lee Grafton asked Sean Rock when Rock returned to the cantina.

"He's in his room."

"Which one?"

"Four."

"That's fine," Lee said. "Sit down, Sean."

Rock did as he was told, and sat with the two remaining Grafton brothers.

"Which two men did you send out to stand watch?" Lee asked.

"I sent Tucker and Lane."

"And who was it who spotted this West coming towards town?"

"Well . . . it was me."

"You're in charge of the men, aren't you?"

"That's right."

Lee sat forward and shouted, "What the fuck happened to Tucker and Lane? Were they asleep?"

"I don't know, Lee."

"Well, find out!" Lee said. "I want to know how West got past them without one of them coming back to town to tell us about him."

"All right, Lee," Rock said, "sure, I'll find out. I'll

send someone out to bring them back."

"Send somebody who won't get lost," Lee said, in a calmer tone, "like they have."

"Sure," Rock said, starting to get up.

"Wait a minute," Lee said. "Before you go, tell me what you think of West."

Rock sat back down and looked from Lee to Wade, and back. "I don't think we need him."

"Why not?" Lee asked. "Because he can shoot better than you?"

"Anybody can shoot at a bunch of glasses," Rock said, uncomfortably.

"You don't like him, do you?"

"No."

"Good," Lee said. "I want you to keep an eye on him."

"What for?"

"Because I don't trust him yet."

"What am I looking for?"

"Anything that doesn't look right," Lee said. "If you see something you don't like, you let me know. Do you understand?"

"Sure, Lee, I understand."

"And don't react out of jealousy, Sean," Lee said, gripping Rock's wrist tightly. "Watch him good, but don't bother me if he's fucking the whore you like."

"I'll watch him good, Lee."

"Okay," Lee said, "now go and take care of that other thing."

Rock stood up and left, rubbing his wrist where Lee had clamped down on it.

"Rock's been with you a long time, Lee," Wade said.

"So?" Lee said, his eyes challenging his brother. "You

saying you don't like the way I treat him?"

"He's your right hand. It wouldn't hurt to treat him with a little more respect."

"I treat him the way I have to, to get what I want from him. You aren't about to start telling me how to treat my men, are you, Wade?"

"No, Lee," Wade said, backing off, "I'm not."

"Good," Lee said. "That's good, Wade."

Sean Rock was fuming.

Generally, he was used to the way Lee Grafton treated him. He had been with Lee longer than anyone, and he knew that Lee valued him, but now this West was here. Lee had hidden it well, but Rock could tell that Lee was impressed with the man.

Maybe Lee was looking to replace Sean Rock with Rick West? No, if that was the case, why would Lee have told Rock to keep an eye on West?

The questions were making Rock's head spin. He wasn't used to heavy thinking, he was used to heavy action.

He'd watch West, all right. He'd watch him good and close.

After a half an hour Clint decided that he couldn't stay in his room forever. There were still several hours before dark, and a couple of hours after that before it would be dark enough for Scarlet to try to come into town unnoticed. Clint couldn't stay in his room all that time.

He decided to take a turn around town and check things out. Lee Grafton had said he had twenty-three men with him in town, but that didn't mean he had twenty-three. Before Clint and Scarlet could make any kind of move, they'd have to know as closely as possible how many men Lee Grafton had in Domingo.

Clint left his room, went downstairs, and stepped out onto the street. He knew he was being watched, he just didn't know by who. He'd be able to figure that out soon enough, though. He knew he was being watched because that was what he would have done if he was Lee Grafton. You don't accept a new man right away. You keep an eye on him and watch him closely.

That wasn't going to make meeting Scarlet after dark very easy.

TWENTY-FOUR

Clint made a circuit of the town, which didn't take long. Domingo wasn't much of a town—not by Texas standards, anyway.

By his count he came up with nineteen men. They weren't doing much, Grafton's men, just hanging around. Some of them were sitting on chairs in front of stores, some were walking, some were standing around, talking to each other. They looked at Clint curiously, but obviously the word had gotten around that there was a new man. They didn't brace him. Neither did they accost him, either verbally or physically. As the new man, he should have been subject to some sort of initiation, yet they left him alone.

They must have been told to leave him alone.

It didn't take Clint long to find out who was following him. Sean Rock was not making much of an attempt to keep from being seen. Grafton had chosen well. Rock had taken an instant dislike to Clint. It was a natural choice to have Rock follow him, and keep an eye on him. Rock would be only too glad to report something to Lee Grafton that would get Clint killed.

Clint passed Domingo's whorehouse, dodging the advances of two Mexican girls who were standing at the front door. He imagined some of Grafton's men were inside. Counting the nineteen he'd seen, plus Rock, plus the Grafton brothers, that made twenty-two that he knew of. He was sure now that there were more than twenty-three, but he didn't know how many more.

He and Scarlet knew they were going to be at a big disadvantage. It was going to be his sad duty to tell her just *how* big.

That is, if he could manage to shake Sean Rock—and he thought he knew of a way to do that.

Clint entered the cantina and saw the Graftons sitting together.

"Am I allowed?" he asked.

Lee Grafton turned and looked at him. "Rick! Come on in. Have a drink."

"I wasn't sure your men were allowed to come in here for a drink," Clint said. "I mean, I don't see any of them around."

"Well, it's true I don't like to have anyone around when I'm in here," Lee said. "They're not a very smart bunch, but they're smart enough to know that."

"I'll leave, then—"

"No, no, no," Lee said, waving at him. "Come on in and have a drink. You've got something the others don't."

"What's that?"

"You're smart," Lee said. "I said that before. It's a pleasure to talk to a smart man, an intelligent man."

Clint told the bartender to draw him a beer, then took it to the table where the Graftons were sitting and joined them.

"Your man Rock is outside," Clint said, settling into his chair. "He's following me . . . on your orders, of course."

"Of course," Lee said. "You've got to keep an eye on a smart man, don't you?"

"Until you come to trust him, I guess."

"Will I?" Lee asked.

"Come to trust me? Probably not."

Lee smiled. He liked that answer. "Why not?"

"You can trust the others, because they're not smart enough for you to worry about," Clint said. "They know they can't make as much money as they can with you."

"And you?"

"Me? Well, you've been saying it all along. I'm smart, and that's exactly why you'll never come to trust me. You might use me for a while, but at some point you'll probably try to kill me."

"And what will happen?"

Clint shrugged. "Either you'll kill me, or I'll kill you."

"Aren't you afraid I'll just have you killed?" Lee asked.

"I don't think you'd do that," Clint said. "I think you'd do it yourself."

"Yes," Lee said, folding his hands in front of him, "yes, I would." He looked at his brother and said, "What do you think, Wade? Would it be interesting?"

"Very interesting."

Clint looked at Wade and decided to be blunt with the man. "What happened to you?"

Wade looked surprised. "What do you mean?"

"I can see the way you move you've been hurt recently. Shot?"

"Yes," Lee said, answering for his brother. "He was shot not long ago."

"By who?"

"A bounty hunter," Lee said, "a bounty hunter who killed our other two brothers, and wounded Wade."

"Ah . . ."

"The bounty hunter should be on the way here, trailing Wade," Lee said.

"And you're waiting for him?"

"Yes."

"What about this job—"

"That will have to wait," Lee said. "My brother and I have other business."

"I can understand that."

"Can you?" Lee asked. "You have any brothers?"

"No."

"Any family?"

Clint hesitated, then said, "No."

"Then you can't understand, can you."

Clint had lost people close to him, people he loved, but he was Rick West now, so he said, "I guess I can't."

He finished his beer and stood up.

"Where are you going?"

"I think I'll check out the local whorehouse. Do they have anything good over there?"

"I wouldn't know," Lee said. "I have my own private stock at the hotel."

Clint knew then that Lee Grafton's room was Room Eight, and that the woman with the melon breasts was his—although she certainly hadn't acted like she was his woman.

"Well, then," Clint said, starting for the batwing doors,

"I'll have to let you know if they have anything good, won't I?"

"Sure," Lee said. "Check out the stock, but be ready when I need you."

Clint turned and looked at Lee. "For what?"

"You might be of some help to us," Lee said, "when the bounty hunter shows up."

Clint studied Lee for a moment, to see if there was any hidden meaning in the man's words. "I'll be around."

TWENTY-FIVE

Clint went to the whorehouse with a specific idea of the kind of whore he wanted. As he entered he was approached by three fresh-faced, firm-bodied young whores, all of whom he waved away.

A heavyset woman in her fifties, with one chin too many, came up to him and said, "Hey, gringo, you come here and you turn my girls down?"

"Do you own this place?"

"Of course I own it," the madam said. "Do you think I would be here otherwise?"

"Well, I'm looking for a certain kind of a woman," Clint said.

"Ah, you want a blonde? I have a blonde, with very white skin. She is upstairs now, but she will be down soon."

"No, I don't want a blonde."

"Aye, then what do you want, then?"

"Why don't I just look around until I find what I want?"

"*Sí, sí,* look around all you want, but if you take up my girls' time and do not take one upstairs, there will still be a fee when you leave."

"Don't worry," he said, "I'll take one upstairs."

In every whorehouse there was the kind of whore he was looking for, and it took him ten minutes to find her in this place.

She was seated on a divan in between two men. They looked like they were two of Grafton's men, dusty hardcases with more balls than brains. Whatever they were talking about, she wasn't interested.

She was in her late thirties, and Clint guessed that she had been at this game for a while. She was still in it because there was nothing else she knew, but she was tired of it and would probably have given anything for a night off.

Clint was going to give her that night.

He moved closer, and she looked up and noticed him. Her dark hair was piled high, and her breasts were pushed up in her dress—probably because they had started to sag, not much, but enough to put her livelihood in danger if it showed. Once she had a customer liquored up and in her room and she was naked, he'd swear she was the most beautiful woman in the world.

"Are you busy?" he asked her.

She had very dark eyes, and naturally dark eyebrows. Her eyes had probably always been her best feature. They were very lovely—but they were probably even lovelier years ago, before the cynicism had crept into them.

"Do I look busy?" she asked. Her English was not heavily accented—probably from servicing a lot of gringos over the years.

"Hey," one of the men said, "we're talkin' to the lady."

"Yeah," his friend said.

"Well, that's the problem, friend," Clint said. "You're talking, and I want to do more than talk."

He put his hand out to the woman and she took it, allowing him to help her to her feet.

"I don't believe it," she said, eyeing him up and down, "a gentleman."

"Hey," the first man said, struggling to get to his feet. The cushions were deep, and he was pretty liquored up already, so Clint just reached out and pushed him back down before he had a chance to make much progress.

"Do yourself a favor, friend," Clint said. "Stay put, and find another girl to bore."

The man squinted at Clint, and seemed about to make another attempt at rising when his friend reached over and slapped him on the shoulder.

"Come on, Lew," he said. "There's other gals here, and plenty younger than this one."

"You said it."

The woman looked at Clint and asked, "Do you want a younger woman?"

"There's a lot to be said for experience," he said to her. "And besides, you don't look so old."

"I've got a lot of miles on me, gringo," she said, putting her hands on her hips. Once they were fine hips, but now they could be described as "ample."

"What's your name, *chica?*"

"Rosa."

"Well, Rosa, if you'd prefer that I spend the entire night with another woman, just say so."

"The entire night?" she asked. She was sharp enough to know that a man couldn't go *all* night, and if she went with him she'd be able to get some sleep. She grabbed his hand and said, "Come this way."

She led him across the room to where the madam was sitting, laughing with a couple of old Mexicans.

"Rosa?" the madam said.

"All night," Rosa said.

"Ah," the madam said, happily, "and do you have the money for all night, *señor*?"

"I work for Lee Grafton."

The woman nodded and said, "Good night, Rosa. See you in the morning."

Rosa grabbed Clint's hand and said, "Good night, Consuela."

TWENTY-SIX

Rosa fairly dragged Clint to the stairway, up the stairs, down the hall, and into her room. Outside her window Clint could see darkness falling. When he looked back at her she already had her dress down to her waist. He'd done her a disservice. She still had very lovely, full breasts, with dark-brown nipples and smooth, rounded undersides. They sagged slightly, but not seriously.

While he was staring at her breasts she got her dress off the rest of the way. There was a slight roll around her middle, and her hips had started to spread. She put her hands up over her head, lifting and jutting her breasts, and did a slow turn around for him. Her butt was full and wide, but not unattractive, and her thighs were probably heavier than they'd ever been. She had told the truth. She had a lot of miles on her, but she still looked like she could do the job.

Unfortunately, Clint wasn't interested in her job at the moment.

She moved closer to him and began to unbutton his shirt. He could feel the heat emanating from her body, and his body began to react.

"Rosa," he said, "I did not come up here to have sex with you."

She pouted at him, slid her hand inside his shirt, and said sadly, "You do not want me?"

"Well, yes—"

"Ah . . ."

"But no."

"What?" She frowned at him, putting her hands on her hips. "Is this a joke?"

"No, it is not a joke," he said. "Look, I will still pay you what Madam Consuela wants, plus something extra for you."

She studied him suspiciously now and said, "And you do not want to sleep with me?"

"No."

"You do not want to beat me, do you?"

"No, I don't want to beat you."

Now she looked puzzled. "Then what do you want?"

"I want to use your window."

"My window?"

"Yes, your window."

Now she was really puzzled.

Outside the whorehouse, Sean Rock was standing across the street. He had seen Rick West go inside, but he had thought it wiser not to follow him in. He decided to settle into a doorway, keep an eye on the front door of the cathouse, and wait for West to come back out.

"I do not understand," Rosa said as Clint walked to her window and looked outside. He was in luck. There was a low roof just outside, and he'd be able to drop down to the ground.

"Look," he said, taking money out of his pocket, "here, take this."

"B-but . . . this is too much."

"I want everyone to think that you and I are up here together, but what I really want to do is go out the window and . . . and meet someone else."

"Who?" she asked. With bills in both hands she put her hands on her hips and asked, "Is she more beautiful than me?"

"It's . . . Juanita. Do you know Juanita?"

Rosa put both her hands to her mouth. "She is Señor Lee Grafton's woman."

"That's right."

"And you are meeting her?"

"Yes."

"Ayee," she said. "You take your life in your hands for her."

"Yes."

Now she lifted her chin and said, "Because she is more beautiful than I?"

Clint took Rosa by the shoulders—round shoulders that were disconcertingly smooth and warm to the touch—and said, "It is not her beauty I crave, Rosa . . . it is the danger."

"Ayee," she said, her eyes lighting up, "now I understand."

"And while I am away," he said, "you can go to sleep . . . all night."

"To sleep . . . all night?" she asked.

"All you have to do is leave your window open so I can come back in the morning—and no one will know what we did."

"Sleep all night," she said, dreamily.

"Yes. Is it a bargain?"

She thought a moment, then looked at the money in both her hands.

"It is a bargain, *señor*."

"Rosa, I am putting my life in your hands. If Lee Grafton finds out, he will kill me."

"He will not find out from me, *señor*," she said, solemnly. "I swear it."

"I believe you," he said. He slid her window open, looked outside, and then put one foot outside.

"Good night, Rosa," he said. "Pleasant dreams."

Rosa watched him climb from the window, then pulled down the covers of her bed and climbed in, taking the money with her.

Maybe, for the first time in a long time, she *would* have pleasant dreams.

TWENTY-SEVEN

Scarlet rubbed her face vigorously with both hands, trying to get her circulation going, trying to wake herself. As she'd waited there for hours, exhaustion had crept over her body, taking control of it, and sleep now pressed at the backs of her eyes.

She stood up and jumped around a bit, shaking her arms and her legs. At one point she saw her horse staring at her, and she stopped.

"No," she said to the animal, "I'm not crazy."

The horse kept staring at her.

"Well, I'm about to ride into a town that might be crawling with killers, with only one man to back me up, so maybe I am crazy. Then again, that one man *is* Clint Adams, so maybe I'm not so crazy. What do you think?"

The horse continued to stare at her for a moment, then looked away. She realized that he was looking in the direction of the town.

"Right," she said, looking at the rapidly darkening sky, "it's time to go."

Now the problems really started.

Clint had to make sure that Scarlet wasn't seen approaching the town, but the moon was already out, and it was damn near full. From a rooftop, somebody was bound to see her, even if she was walking her horse.

That meant that he had to take care of the men on the rooftops—and he had to kill them. He couldn't afford taking the chance that one of them might revive and sound the alarm. Of course, in killing them he took the chance of their bodies being discovered—perhaps by someone who was relieving one of them—but that was a chance he was going to have to take, for Scarlet's sake. She was coming into town on his say-so that she'd be safe, and he couldn't just leave her out there as an easy target.

He remembered which roofs were manned as he rode into town, and he hoped that the same ones were still being manned.

After leaving Rosa's window he had remained on that low roof for a while, watching the alley below. Craning his head to his left, he could see the main street. He waited for darkness before he took the chance of dropping down off the low roof.

Finally, he slid down to the edge, almost slipping at one point on a loose roof shingle. He managed to pin it to the roof with his foot so that it wouldn't slide to the edge and fall over, and then picked it up. He wedged it against another shingle so that it wouldn't move.

When he reached the end he saw that the drop was only about ten feet. He was six feet tall, so hanging by his hands he would be only four feet from the ground. He would also be in a pretty defenseless position at that moment, but that couldn't be helped.

He lowered himself over the edge of the roof, hung there just an instant, and then released his hands. . . .

• • •

Scarlet rode for a short distance, and then by the light of the nearly full moon she spied the town. She halted her horse, dismounted, and began to walk, trailing the animal behind her. It might have been smarter to release the horse there, but the animal might have smelled water, or food, or other horses, and headed straight for town.

She wondered what she'd find ahead. Was the town harmless, and would Clint Adams be waiting with a hot meal? Or was the town full of killers, with Clint Adams already dead?

No, she couldn't think that way. She had to keep going, and depend on Clint to keep her from being seen.

She had to have faith in him, even though there was a chill at the base of her spine that just wouldn't go away.

Jerry Crider had relieved Ted Kerns only an hour earlier, when there was still some light in the sky. Now, he felt it was useless for him to keep staring out across the flat. Nobody in their right mind would be riding out there at night, and even if they were, he couldn't make out who they were. How was he supposed to know if someone approaching the town had red hair or not? Look for somebody with red hair, they'd told him. Sounded damned stupid to him.

He heard a noise behind him, but turned a little too late. Somebody took hold of his head and helped him turn it the rest of the way, real quick.

There was a loud snap, and Jerry Crider didn't have to worry about anything stupid anymore.

Clint lowered the man's body to the roof, then stared over at the other roof. He could barely make out the silhouette of the man over there. He looked out across the flat. Did he really see someone walking out there, or was he imagining it?

He had to get to the other roof, and fast.

TWENTY-EIGHT

Scarlet could feel the tension throughout her whole body. She was an easy target out here, and she kept waiting for a hot chunk of lead to rip through her body.

Trust Clint, she kept telling herself, just trust Clint. . . .

The street was empty, which was probably the only bit of luck Clint would see that night. He crossed quickly to the other building, and worked his way around to the back. There was a low-hanging roof there and he managed to grip the edge and pull himself up. It would have been easier from the inside, but he didn't want to take a chance on breaking into the building. The first level was a store, but the second level might have been someone's home.

The flat adobe wall had long wooden pegs sticking out of it. What they were for he didn't know, but they were just what he needed to scale the wall and get to the roof.

He jumped up, caught one, and pulled himself up.

Across the street from the whorehouse Sean Rock was lighting a cigarette. He wondered how long Rick West would spend inside. He wouldn't have minded spending some time in Consuela's himself, and if West would just come out and go back to his room for the night, he could do that.

Jesus, he thought then, what if he's going to spend the whole damn night in there?

"What are you thinking about?" Wade Grafton asked his brother.

"Lots of things," Lee said. "That bitch bounty hunter, for one. If she's any good she ought to be here by now."

"What if she lost my trail?"

"If she doesn't ride in by tomorrow, we're going to have to go looking for her," Lee said. "I want to get her out of the way before we go ahead with the job."

"By the way," Wade said, "what is the job?"

Lee looked at his brother and said, "You know better than that. You'll find out when everybody else does, same as always."

"Is this a big one, Lee?"

"It's a big one, Wade," Lee said. "Even Harley and Sam couldn't have spent all the money they would have made from this one all in one place."

And now, Wade thought, their share would be split between Lee and him. Half of the take always went to the brothers, with the rest going to whatever other men they had used. Now, the full brothers' share would go to Lee and Wade.

Was that worth losing his brothers? Wade wondered.

Well, he told himself realistically, that would depend on how much money they were talking about.

Wouldn't it?

Lee Grafton was also thinking about Rick West. He didn't like a stranger riding into town right before a big job, announcing that he wanted to join. Lee had sent word out long ago that he had all the men he needed. Where had Rick West heard about this, and hadn't he heard that part of it? Maybe he had, and still wanted to join up. Lee had to admit that he wished he had more men of Rick West's ilk, but they were a rare commodity.

Too damned rare to have one come riding into town right out of nowhere.

Clint reached the top of the roof and crept up behind the man, hoping there was nothing on the roof he could step on, into, or trip over.

"What the—" he heard the man say to himself. "There's somebody out there."

Clint moved closer.

The man turned towards the other roof and started to shout, "Hey—"

Clint ran up on him then and caught him before he could say anything else. He slid his arm around the man's neck, beneath the chin, and clamped down. The man dropped the rifle he was holding and started to fight, but Clint had one knee wedged into the small of the man's back as he increased the pressure on the man's throat. He was cutting off the man's air completely, and after a few more seconds of struggling the man stopped and went limp. Clint kept the pressure on a bit longer, to make sure the man was dead, and then lowered him to the floor.

Clint stood up and looked out over the flat. Now he could clearly see someone walking, trailing a horse behind.

It was Scarlet, and he had to get out there to meet her.

• • •

Scarlet had her eyes fixed on the town, and when she saw a man approaching her from there, on foot, with no horse in sight, she dropped her right hand down by her gun. She couldn't see his face. He walked like Clint, and looked like him, but until she could see his face, she would stay ready.

Finally, the man got close enough for her to see his face, and it was Clint Adams.

"Jesus," she said, as he reached her. "You scared me silly."

"Come on," he said, grabbing her arm. "We've got to go this way and approach the town from an angle."

"Are they there?" she asked.

He didn't answer fast enough for her and she tore her arm loose from his hold.

"Are they there, Clint?"

"Yes, they're there," he hissed. "Keep your voice down."

"Are there lookouts?"

"Two. I took care of them," he said, taking her arm again, "but their bodies could be discovered at any time."

"Well, what are we gonna do now?" she asked. "If you've already killed two of them, they'll know something is wrong soon."

"I know, I know," Clint said. "I'm thinking."

"How many men are we dealing with?" she asked. "How big a gang?"

"More than twenty."

"Twenty?" she said. "That's not a gang, it's a damned army."

He stopped and turned to face her. She had been trotting, trying to keep up with his pace, and when he turned she started and bumped into him.

"You want to pull out, Scarlet? We still have time, you know."

"No," she said, without hesitation. "We're going ahead."

He started at her for a moment, then said, "All right, then. Let's keep going before someone spots us."

He started walking again at the same pace, and she had to hurry to keep up.

"Have you met them?"

"Yes."

"Well, what did you tell them? Who did you say you were?"

"We can go over that when we're under some cover, Scarlet," he said. "Out here we're easy targets. Now quiet down until we find someplace to talk."

She opened her mouth to say something, but they were so close to the town now that she could hear music.

She kept quiet, but the questions were piling up in her mind.

TWENTY-NINE

"Get me someone."

Wade looked at his brother and said, "What?"

"I said get me someone," Lee said. "Anyone. I want to find West."

Wade frowned, but stood up and walked to the cantina doors. There was usually one or two men hanging about, just in case Lee wanted something. He looked outside and saw a man sitting in a wooden chair. The chair was propped up against the wall of the cantina, and the man was dozing.

"Hey!" Wade called.

The man came awake, and the front legs of the chair fell to the boardwalk. "What?"

"What's your name?"

"Um, Jeff," the man said. "Jeff Jacks."

He was barely twenty, but he was old enough for the errand Lee had in mind.

"Come inside. Lee wants you."

"Me?" Jacks said, looking surprised.

Wade pointed and said, "You."

Wade turned and reentered the cantina, with Jeff Jacks in tow.

"This is Jeff," Wade said. "Jeff Jacks."

Lee looked up at the young man, who was looking down at Lee with wide eyes.

"I didn't know we were taking kids," Lee said to no one in particular. The fact of the matter was, he remembered accepting Jacks into the gang.

"I ain't a kid, Mr. Grafton," Jacks said. "I'm twenty."

"Can you do a job for me, Jeff?"

"Sure I can."

"Did you see the man who rode into town today?"

"Yes, sir."

"His name is Rick West."

"I know, sir."

"At least," Lee said, again to no one in particular, "he says that's his name. Anyway, I want you to find him."

"Find him?"

"Yes," Lee said. "Find him."

"Uh, where would I start to look . . . sir?"

"Well," Lee said, "when he left here he was headed for Consuela's."

"T-the whorehouse?" Jacks said, his voice cracking.

Lee looked at Jacks with amusement. "That's right, the whorehouse. If he's not there, check the hotel, Room Four. Find him and tell him I want him. Got it?"

"Yessir, I got it."

As Jacks headed for the door Lee called out, "Look for Sean Rock. He's supposed to be following West."

"Yessir," Jacks said, and was out the door.

"Does what he's told, doesn't he?" Lee said.

"What do you want with West, Lee?"

"I want to talk to him some more," Lee said. "I want to see if he slips up on his story."

"And if he doesn't?"

"Then he'll ride on the job with us."

"And if he does slip up?"

"Then maybe I'll let young Jacks there kill him."

"No," Wade said. "West was right about that. You'll kill him yourself."

"Yeah," Lee said, "I guess I will. I haven't killed anyone in weeks."

Jeff Jacks ran down the street towards the whorehouse, but before he crossed the street he noticed Sean Rock standing in a doorway.

"Mr. Rock?"

"That's right," Rock said, giving the younger man an annoyed look. "What's your name, boy?"

"Jeff, sir," Jacks said. "Jeff Jacks."

"What are you doin' out and about?" Rock said. "Why ain't you in Consuela's—or ain't you ever been with a whore?"

Rock laughed, but the boy wouldn't be deterred from his errand.

"Mr. Grafton sent me down here."

Rock stopped laughing and frowned. "Lee?"

"Yessir."

"What for?"

"He asked me to find Mr. West. He said if I found you I'd find him."

"Well, you've found both of us," Rock said. He jerked his chin in the direction of the whorehouse and said, "He's in there."

"Well, Mr. Grafton wants him over to the cantina now," Jacks said.

"He does, huh?" Rock said. Maybe Lee had seen the light and was gonna kill West.

Rock pushed himself out of the doorway and slapped Jacks on the back. "Well, then, I guess we better go get him, huh, kid?"

"Yessir."

Together they crossed the street to the whorehouse and entered it.

THIRTY

"So what are you telling me?" Scarlet asked. "That it's hopeless?"

"No," Clint answered, "I'm not saying that."

"What are you saying, then?"

Clint and Scarlet—and Scarlet's horse—were behind an adobe building, in the shadows and, hopefully, totally out of sight. Clint and Scarlet literally had their backs up against the wall, and were huddling on what their next move would be.

"What I'm saying," Clint said, "is that it's a next-to-impossible situation."

"Then how do we go about making it possible?"

"Well," Clint said, "as I see it, what we want to accomplish here is to take Lee and Wade Grafton out of Domingo without having to face twenty-three or so armed men."

"Dead or alive."

"What?"

"We want to take them dead or alive," she said.

Clint frowned, opened his mouth to protest, then closed it.

"Ideally," he said, "we should take them dead."

Scarlet looked at him in surprise. Although they were standing shielded from the moon, in total darkness, their night vision was such that they could make out each other's expressions.

"I'm surprised to hear you say that," she said.

"Don't be," Clint said. "What's keeping Grafton's men here is the promise of a big job and a lot of money."

"So? They're certainly not going to let us take him easy then."

"No," Clint said, "but they might just let us take him— them—dead."

"If we kill them you think the other men are just going to let us leave?"

"Why not?" Clint asked. "With Lee Grafton dead, who knows what job he was planning? How are they going to get paid the money that's been promised them?"

Scarlet thought a moment, then said, "You might have a point."

"Then again," Clint said, "they might just kill us out of disappointment."

Scarlet looked exasperated and said, "So then we're back where we started, with a next-to-hopeless situation on our hands."

Clint was rubbing his jaw as something occurred to him.

"Maybe not," he said. "There might just be a way for us to take the other men out of the picture."

"There *might* be a way?" she asked. "How will we know for sure?"

"For that," Clint said, pushing away from the wall, "we need one of Grafton's men. Come on."

Inside the whorehouse Sean Rock sought out Consuela. The chubby madam saw him coming towards her and plastered a professional smile on her face. She knew Rock as Grafton's right-hand man, and treated him accordingly. She had never charged him for a whore.

"Señor Rock," she said, but Rock let her get no further.

"Consuela, where's West?"

"Who?"

"The new man, Rick West."

"I still do not know your men all by name, Señor Rock," she said, "and if this gringo is a new man . . ." She paused and shrugged her shoulders helplessly.

Impatiently, Rock described Clint as well as he possibly could, and Consuela's eyes showed recognition.

"Ah, now I know who you mean," she said, happily. "That gringo took Rosa upstairs."

"For how long?"

"All night."

"All night?" Rock said. "Isn't Rosa your oldest whore?"

"She has been with me the longest, yes."

"There are other, younger women he could have taken for all night," Rock said. "Why her?"

"I do not know, *señor*," Consuelo said. "Perhaps he appreciates experience."

"Which room is hers?"

"Room Five, *señor*," Consuelo said, frowning. "Will there be trouble?"

He ignored her and said to Jacks, "Come on."

Jacks, who had never been in the whorehouse before, was ogling all of the scantily clad whores, and started when Rock nudged him.

Rock led the way to the stairs and up. Impatiently, he found the door to Room Five and tried the doorknob. It was locked, and he lifted his right leg and slammed it open with a well-placed kick.

Rosa sat bolt upright in bed, her sheet dropping to her waist.

What Jeff Jacks noticed was her full, rounded breasts with their dark nipples, and he felt an immediate tightening in his groin.

What Sean Rock noticed was that Rosa was in bed alone and Rick West was nowhere to be found. He felt an immediate tightening at his temples as his head started to pound. He had been tricked but good, and was now going to have to explain it to Lee Grafton.

THIRTY-ONE

"What's your plan?" Scarlet asked.

They were walking along behind the buildings, still sticking to the shadows. They had left Scarlet's horse tethered behind that first building, hoping the animal would keep quiet.

"It's simple," he said. "At any given time there's a good number of Grafton's men in the whorehouse. If we can catch them there unawares, we can immobilize them all at one time."

"How many are we talking about?"

Clint shrugged and said, "I don't know. Seven, eight, maybe ten at one time."

"Well," she said, "that does decrease the odds some, but they're still bad."

"There's something else."

"What?"

"Grafton has cleared out the cantina, and when he drinks there he doesn't like any of his men around. Usually, there's him and his brother there, with some men loitering outside and maybe Sean Rock—his right-hand man—inside with the Graftons."

"So? We should head for the cantina, then."

"No," Clint said. "There's still the chance an alarm

153

will be sounded, and then we'll be trapped inside."

"With the Graftons," she said. "We can hold them hostage and get out. You said yourself that Grafton is the only one who knows what his big job is. They won't let us kill him."

"No," Clint said. "A situation like that would be too volatile. Something could easily go wrong."

"Then what do you suggest?"

"I was coming to that," he said, and she fell silent so he could continue. "Since Grafton allows no one in the cantina, if I was one of his men who was going to have to be waiting in this town for weeks, I'd set up a saloon somewhere else."

"You mean, his men would set up their own saloon?"

"Sure," Clint said. "They could stock it from the cantina, and set it up in another building somewhere. If that's the case, then we could catch another eight or ten of them there."

"And if we did that, we'd really cut down on the odds," she said.

"Right."

"Then we've got to find out if they've done that."

"Which means we need one of his men."

"Where are we going now?"

"The whorehouse," Clint said. "We might as well put this plan into action right now."

Sean Rock stayed with Rosa and sent Jeff Jacks to fetch Lee Grafton. He figured he might as well let Lee talk to the woman himself.

"*Señor,*" Rosa said, "I can get dressed?"

"No," he said. "You stay right where you are, bitch. You got a lot of explaining to do."

"I do not understand," she said.

"You will," he said. "You will."

Rosa, under Rock's hard gaze, reached for the sheet and pulled it up to her throat. Rock reached out, grabbed the sheet at the bottom, and yanked it off her and the bed in one motion. He took in her body, the extra pounds that had come with age, the dark hair between her legs, and shook his head.

"You're turning into a real pig, ain't you?" he said. "You been at this game a long time?"

Trying to hide herself with her hands, she said, "A long time, *señor.*"

"Jesus," Rock said. "Is there anything worse than an old whore?"

She felt ashamed, but she felt something even more intense. She *hated* Sean Rock for doing this to her, and stared at him with hot eyes.

Given half a chance, she thought that she would enjoy killing this gringo.

Lee Grafton did not take kindly to Sean Rock sending *his* messenger back to him with a message. However, he changed his mind when he heard what Jeff Jacks had to say.

"You go over to the hotel, Jacks, and see if West is there. Maybe he got past Rock."

"Yessir."

"I'll come with you," Wade said, starting to rise.

"No, stay here, Wade," Lee said. "I'll take care of this myself."

Wade admitted to himself that he would rather stay at the cantina, so he didn't argue with his brother. Truth be told, sitting there drinking with Lee had lulled him into a sleepy state, and he was too lazy to even get up from his chair to go to bed.

"Get moving!" Lee Grafton shouted at Jacks.

"Yessir!"

The younger man hurried out of the cantina, followed by Lee Grafton, who was moving swiftly and determinedly.

THIRTY-TWO

When they reached the back of the whorehouse something else occurred to Clint, and he stopped at the back door.

"What is it?" Scarlet asked.

"Stay here a minute," he said.

She started to protest, but he slipped away in the dark, leaving her alone. She could have followed him, but she chose to stay and wait.

Clint moved along the alley outside of Rosa's room, and looked up at her window. The light was still burning. He continued on until he got to the end of the alley, and peered out at the main street. If Sean Rock thought he was still inside the whorehouse, he would have still been outside, waiting for Clint to come out.

He scanned the doorways across the street, but could find no sign of Rock. There was no glow of a cigarette, and no impatient movement from the shadows.

Rock wasn't there. Why not? There was no way he could know that Rick West was staying the night. Why would Rock abandon his position? Until he knew that Clint was no longer inside.

At that moment Clint saw Lee Grafton walking down the street towards the whorehouse, and he recognized the mood of the man from his pace.

Something was wrong.

He turned and hurried back to Scarlet to tell her what he thought.

"Then our plan is ended before it even starts," she said. "They know you're not upstairs."

"Maybe, but they still don't know where I am."

"So what do we do? Hide?"

"You hide," Clint said. "I've got an idea."

"Where do I hide?"

"Go back to where your horse is and stay behind that building. If something goes wrong, if you hear a commotion, or if you hear shots, get on your horse and ride."

"And leave you?"

"There won't be anything you can do for me, Scarlet," Clint said. "You'll have to get away so you can stay alive to figure out something else. Do you understand?"

"I don't like it," she said stubbornly.

"You don't have to like it," he said. "All you have to do is understand it."

"I understand it, damn you. I'm not a fool."

Clint hoped not.

He took her by the shoulders and said, "This could still work. I've got a pretty daring idea, and if I can make it work, we could still get the Graftons. Trust me a little longer, okay?"

She stared at him, then impulsively hugged him tightly and said, "Okay."

Grafton ignored the whores and men in the parlor and mounted the steps.

"Rock?"

"In here, boss," Rock said, sticking his head out of Room Five.

Grafton entered Room Five and saw the naked whore on the bed. "What's going on?"

"Consuela says West was spending the whole night with this whore," Rock said. "As you can see, he ain't here."

"I can see that," Grafton said, impatiently. He looked at the whore and said, "Where is West?"

"I do not know this West."

"The man who came up here with you," Grafton said, moving closer to the bed. "Where is he, whore?"

She shrank back from him and her eyes flicked to the window. She also kept her hands jammed down tightly on her pillow.

Grafton moved to the window and said to Rock, "See what she's hiding under the pillow."

He looked outside the window and saw the low roof. Why would West pay for a night with a whore, and then climb out the window?

He heard the sound of a resounding slap and then Rock's voice said, "Money, Lee."

Grafton turned and saw Rock holding money in his hands. The girl was holding both of her hands to her face, rocking on the bed and crying silently.

"More than she's worth," Rock added.

"Leave it," Grafton said.

"What?"

"Leave the money."

Rock frowned, but he released the money and it fluttered to the bed and the floor. Rosa began to hastily pick it up.

"He pays for a night with a whore, and goes out the window," Grafton said. He looked at Rock and said, "Why?"

"He ain't what he seems, Lee. I knew that from the start."

"Take a few men and start searching," Lee said.

"I could have all the men cover the whole town, Lee," Rock said. "We could smoke him out—"

"No, I don't want a big commotion," Lee said, cutting Rock off. "Wherever he is, I don't want to tip him off. Do it without making a fuss, understand?"

"Sure, Lee," Rock said, "I understand. I'll find him and bring you his tongue."

Grafton moved close to Rock and pointed a finger at him.

"I want him alive, understand, Sean?" Lee said. "I make the decisions here about who lives and dies. You find him, you bring him to me alive."

"Sure, Boss," Rock said. "Sure."

"I'll be in the cantina," Lee said. "Don't keep me waiting, Rock."

He started for the door, with Rock behind him. In the hall, Lee turned and said, "You were supposed to watch him, Sean. You were supposed to be watching him good. You disappointed me. Don't do it again."

"Boss—"

"Just find him."

They went downstairs, and separated when they reached the first floor. Rock checked the parlor to see who was there, and picked two men to take with him, leaving six or seven still there.

Sean Rock was even angrier now than he had been before. Rick West had really made him look bad now, and he was going to pay him back for it.

He was going to pay him back in triplicate!

THIRTY-THREE

Clint reentered the hotel by the back door and made his way to the second floor. He peered around the corner and saw a young man standing at his door. He was knocking on it, probably for the third or fourth time.

"Shit," the man said. He tried the knob and found it locked. He stood in front of the door, as if he was undecided about what to do next. Finally he turned and walked away, heading for the main stairs. Clint heard him muttering to himself, something about "getting a key."

As the man disappeared from sight Clint entered the hall and walked directly to Room Eight. He knocked, and the door was opened almost immediately.

"Well," Juanita said, "what are you doing here?"

He smiled at her and said, "You mean you didn't want me to come?"

She smiled, and looked up and down the hall.

"Do you know whose room this is?" she asked.

"Yes."

"He could be back any moment."

"He's busy," Clint said. "Besides . . . you look like the kind of woman who likes danger."

161

"*Sí,*" she said, "but I like money more—and I like living even more."

"Juanita—" he began, but he heard footsteps on the stairs, the footsteps of more than one man.

"What—" she said, but he stepped inside, forcing her back, and closed the door.

"What is it?" she asked.

"Shhh."

Outside the room they heard men walking by.

"Why didn't you kick in the door?" a man's voice demanded impatiently. Clint recognized it as that of Sean Rock.

"I didn't know, Mr. Rock," another voice said, lamely.

"That is Rock," Juanita said.

"Yes."

"They are looking for you?"

"Yes."

"To kill you?"

He looked at her and said, "Perhaps."

"If they find you here with me—"

"They will not kill me."

"Lee will."

"No," Clint said, "he won't."

She frowned at him and asked, "Why are you here?"

"I need help."

"No," she said. "Why are you here in Domingo?"

He decided to play it straight with her. He couldn't be in any more danger than he was now.

"I've come to take Lee and his brother Wade back to the United States."

"Ah," she said, "you will arrest him?"

"I will take them back with me and turn them over to the law."

Down the hall they heard the sound of a door being kicked in.

"Hurry," she said suddenly. She pulled her peasant blouse up over her head, and he couldn't help but catch his breath and stare at her pear-shaped breasts.

"Hurry," she said, again, "take off your clothes."

Rock looked around West's room and then turned and kicked the door again.

"He's not here," he said unnecessarily.

The other men—Jacks and, the two Rock had taken from the whorehouse—looked at each other and shrugged.

"I want the hotel searched," Rock said. "Every room."

"Sean," one man said, "most of the rooms are taken by our men."

"Search them!" Rock said. "He's got to be here somewhere. When we're finished with the hotel we'll search the whole town."

"That could take all night," the other man said.

Rock gave them all hard stares and said, "Just do it, damn it!"

THIRTY-FOUR

Rock stood in the hall and waited while the other three men knocked on and kicked in doors.

"There's no sign of him, Sean," one of the men said.

"Did you check all the rooms?"

"All except yours and Mr. Grafton's."

"Mine," Rock said, shaking his head. "Wouldn't that be something? Come on, I'll open it."

He led them down the hall to his room and unlocked the door. They went inside and lit a candle.

"Not here," Rock said.

"That leaves Room Eight," Jeff Jacks said.

All of Grafton's men knew what Room Eight was. That was where Lee kept Juanita.

"Juanita's in there," Rock said.

"Do we look inside?" one of the men asked.

Nervously, Rock tried to decide. If they bothered Juanita, Lee would have his head, but what if West was in there, maybe holding her hostage, or something?

"Sean?" one of the men asked. "Do we?"

Lying in bed with Juanita, Clint heard the men clumping about in the hall.

"It will take them a while to search the hotel," he said.

"Well," Juanita said, "we should not waste that time, should we?"

She slid her hand down over his belly until her hand had encircled him. He had been semi-erect at that point, but now he swelled to bursting.

"Juanita—" he said, protesting.

She put her mouth to his ear, moistening it with her tongue, and said, "If you resist, I will scream."

He looked at her and saw amusement in her eyes. He felt her body pressed tightly against him. Her big, heavy breasts were flattened against him, and he could feel her hard nipples scraping him. Her insistent hand was massaging him, rubbing him up and down, and then it slid down and tickled his testicles.

"Jesus," he said, reaching for her.

"Sean?"

"Yeah, yeah," Rock said, "I'm thinking."

"If he's in there—" one of the men began, but Rock silenced him with a wave of his hand.

"I'm thinking, damn it!"

Inside the room Clint wasn't thinking at all. He was lost in what seemed like acres of Juanita's flesh. He captured her breasts in his hands and lifted them to his mouth, sucking her nipples until she was moaning and writhing beneath him. Her hands were still insistent between them, rubbing his hard column of flesh.

"Oooh, please . . ." she said, spreading her legs, "*por favor . . .*"

He slid a leg over her and entered her, cleaving her easily and sliding home to the hilt. She was hot and wet, and her legs around his hips were powerful. He slid his hands beneath her to cup her big buttocks, and then started slamming into her, setting the bed to squeaking.

Outside the room stood Sean Rock and the other three men, and they could hear the squeaking noise.

"Them are the bedsprings," one of the men said, looking at the others.

"Maybe Grafton is in there with her," the other said.

Jeff Jacks looked at Sean Rock.

"I guess I'll knock," Rock finally said, and lifted his hand to do so.

"Ooooh," Juanita keened, and erupted beneath him. He bounced with her, like a cowpoke trying to stay with a wild bronc. He continued to drive into her, working his way to his own eruption, when there was a knock on the door.

"Lee? You in there?" Sean Rock called.

Clint stopped, but Juanita was lost, continuing to move beneath him. She opened her mouth to moan again, and Clint covered it with his hand.

"Shh," he told her. Her eyes, glazed moments earlier, came into focus. "If he comes in here with his men, there's going to be shooting. I want to avoid that."

He slid his hand away from her mouth and she said, "How?"

"You open the door and invite him in," Clint said. "Just him. Understand?"

"*Sí, señor*," she said, "*comprendo*."

Clint moved, sliding his still-hard penis out of her. She moaned and bit her lip as he moved, then slid to the end of the bed and sat up. She grabbed a thin wrap that was on a chair near the bed and put it on. As she stood up he

could see that the wrap molded itself to her. He could see
the crease between her full buttocks clearly, and when
she turned, the wrap showed the outline of her distended
nipples starkly.

Clint pulled on his pants as Rock knocked again and
said, "Juanita? Is Lee in there?"

Clint held his finger to his lips, then stood up next
to her.

"Tell him you're coming to the door," he whispered,
his mouth pressed to her ear.

"I am coming," she called out, and then bit her lip.
He could see that she was nervous. She was helping him
hide from Grafton's men, and if Lee Grafton found out—
and Clint *didn't* take him—she was going to be in a lot
of trouble.

He looked at her, then readjusted the front of her wrap
so that most of her breasts were showing. She saw what
he was after, and smilingly adjusted it even more so that
some of her brown nipples were showing. He smiled too,
and nodded his approval.

Clint got into bed, pulling the sheet up to cover his
pants. He showed her his gun and then placed it beneath
the sheet with him, hoping that would help her set aside
her fears.

Juanita went to the door and opened it.

THIRTY-FIVE

What Jeff Jacks saw when the door opened beat anything he had seen over at the whorehouse. He had heard about Juanita, but hadn't actually seen her himself. Now he was seeing most of what she had to offer and he knew why Lee Grafton was keeping her to himself.

He swallowed hard.

"What is it . . . Sean?" she asked. She had never used Rock's first name before.

"Uh, we're looking for a man, Juanita. His name is Rick West. Lee isn't in there with you, is he?"

"No, Lee is not here."

Sean tried to see inside, but she closed the door a bit and stood in his way.

"Do you want to come in?" she asked him.

"Well . . . we are supposed to search the whole hotel. Those are Lee's orders."

"I don't want all these men in my room, Sean," she said. "Tell them to go away, and you can come in."

Rock wasn't sure, but there seemed to be invitation in her eyes, and her mouth.

She was the most beautiful woman he had ever seen, and he had always envied Lee.

"Sean?" she said.

"All right," he said. He turned to the other men and said, "I'll look inside. You boys start searching the town, but don't be noisy about it. Lee doesn't want to tip West off that we're looking for him."

The three men exchanged glances, and then Jacks said, "All right, Sean."

"I'll catch up . . . as soon as I'm done here."

Now they exchanged a different kind of glance, then turned and walked away, shaking their heads. Any one of them would have given a lot to be in Sean Rock's shoes right then.

"All right, Juanita," Rock said. "How about letting me in?"

She nodded, smiled, and backed away from the door. Sean Rock entered, his eyes on her, but inside he saw Clint in the bed and froze.

"You're crazy," Rock said.

"Why?"

"Lee will kill you when he finds out."

"And what were you coming in here to do, Rock?" Clint asked.

"I was just searching."

"Sure."

Rock looked over at Juanita, who had closed the wrap to cover herself completely. Clint could tell by the way the man's shoulders tensed that he was going to go for his gun.

"Don't try it," Clint said, and tossed the sheet aside. Rock's eyes widened when he saw that Clint was half dressed and holding his gun.

"You're crazy," Rock said again as Clint got off the bed.

"I don't think so."

"What are you planning to do?"

"My plans are none of your business," Clint said.

"When Lee finds out—"

"He'll find out soon enough," Clint said, "but you aren't going to tell him."

The man's eyes widened again. He interpreted Clint's words to mean that he was going to kill him. He grabbed for his gun, to at least die with it in his hand, but Clint brought the barrel of his own gun down on the man's head and Rock slumped to the floor.

"What will you do now?" Juanita asked.

"I need you to do me another favor," Clint said. He slid his gun into his holster and strapped it on, then reached for his shirt.

"Will it help you arrest Lee Grafton?"

He didn't correct her, but simply said, "Yes."

"Then I will do it."

"Good. Get dressed. At the north end of town, on the west side, there's a red-haired woman waiting behind a building."

"Your woman?" Juanita asked.

"My partner," Clint said. "I want you to tell her what's happening, and tell her I've gone to the whorehouse to begin our plan."

"The whorehouse," Juanita said. "That is because we did not finish?"

He smiled and said, "No, Juanita. You and I will finish another time. I'm going there to take care of Grafton's men."

"But he has others."

"I know. I plan to find them, if I can find out where they do their drinking."

"That is easy," she said. "Because they cannot use the cantina, they have taken over a building at the south end of town."

"The south end? Thank you, Juanita. You've been a big help."

He took her by the shoulders and kissed her. He meant it to be a short kiss, but she released her wrap to put her arms around him and it fell open. She pressed her naked body to him, opening her mouth beneath his, and they kissed deeply for what seemed like forever. Clint was painfully erect again, acutely aware of the fact that they had *not* finished what they were doing when they were interrupted. At least, *he* hadn't finished.

Finally, he pushed her away and said, "Get dressed, Juanita. I'll see you later."

"*Vaya con Dios,*" she said, reaching for her clothes as he moved to the door. "Do not get killed."

"I don't plan on it," he said, but as he left he thought, Who does?

THIRTY-SIX

Clint went directly to the whorehouse, hoping that Scarlet could avoid the searching men until Juanita could get to her.

He forced the back door of the whorehouse and entered. There was still some lively activity going on in the parlor, but he was sure some of Grafton's men would have gone upstairs with some of the girls by now.

He worked his way down the hall to the parlor, and then pulled his gun from his holster and Rock's gun from his belt. He felt that having two guns would make him seem more threatening when he entered the parlor.

He stepped into the parlor and called out, "Give me your attention, please!" He hoped they would, because he couldn't afford to fire a shot to get it.

Luckily, he only had to shout a second time to get everyone's attention.

"You men just stay where you are, and don't try for your guns. If we start shooting in here a lot of people are going to get hurt."

There were about ten men in the room, and Clint felt sure that at least seven of them were Grafton's. The other three might have been, but they could also have been men from town, or *vaqueros* from nearby ranches.

"Girls, get their guns and bring them over to me," Clint instructed.

The whores looked at Consuela, who nodded. She was seated, and seemed perfectly calm.

"Are you here for Lee Grafton?" she asked.

"That's right," Clint said. He told the girls, "Just drop them at my feet like good girls."

"Good," Consuela said. "If you kill him, perhaps we can get back to normal."

"Consuela, I need the cooperation of you and your girls."

"You have it."

"Are any of Grafton's men upstairs?"

"Three."

"I need to have all of these men tied up. Can your girls handle that?"

"Of course," Consuelo said, "but two of these men do not work for Grafton."

"That's all right," he said. "Being tied up will keep them out of harm's way."

"You heard the *señor,* girls," Consuelo said. "Tie them up—and do it right!"

Scarlet heard someone running towards her, and drew her gun. When she saw that it was a woman she became confused for a moment—then she remembered what she herself had said about Clint and women.

"You are Señor West's friend?" Juanita asked.

"West?" she asked, then realized that was probably the name Clint was using. "I'm his partner."

"I have a message," Juanita said.

• • •

When all of the men in the parlor were tied up, Clint went upstairs and fetched Grafton's men one by one. Naked, they were easily taken, and he led them downstairs, where they were also tied up.

That done, Clint holstered his gun.

"Can any of your girls handle a gun?" he asked Consuela.

"Carmella."

Carmella came forward. She was a tiny, dark-eyed girl with breasts too big for her body—some men might say.

"Hold this gun and keep an eye on them," Clint instructed. "I don't think you'll have to use it."

"Do not worry, *señor*," Carmella said, "I shoot very well."

"Just keep them here until I get back," Clint said.

"Do not worry about us, *señor*," Consuela said. "You go and do what you must to rid us of Lee Grafton."

"I'll do my best," he said, and left by the front door.

Outside, he found both Juanita and Scarlet waiting for him.

"I see you two have found each other."

"How did it go inside?" Scarlet asked.

"Fine, we have eleven of his men tied up."

"Did you find their saloon?"

"Yes, thanks to Juanita," Clint said. "She's been a big help to us."

"I'm sure," Scarlet said, wryly. "Shall we go before someone sees us?"

"Juanita," Clint said, "you go inside."

Juanita nodded and said, "Be careful. We have unfinished business."

She went inside, and Scarlet eyed Clint. "Unfinished business?"

"Don't we all?"

They peered inside the window and saw a makeshift bar that had been fashioned by placing some wooden planks on top of two barrels. There was one man behind the bar, and six or seven standing at it. There were no tables in the room, just the stand-up bar.

"Go to the back," Clint said, "and don't enter until I do."

"Right."

He gave her enough time to get around back, then entered with his gun still in his holster.

As he walked in they all turned and looked at him.

"Howdy, boys."

They frowned until one man said, "That's the new man, Rick West."

The others relaxed then, and Clint drew his gun.

"Actually," he said, as Scarlet came through the back door, "the name is Adams, and I'd like you men to put your hands up, please."

They looked at him again, and then they all heard the sound of Scarlet cocking her gun behind them.

"Please," she echoed.

When Clint and Scarlet left the makeshift saloon there were eight men tied up on the floor. Their guns had been dropped out a window into a rain barrel.

"Who's left?" she asked.

"There are three men searching the town for me," Clint said, "and the Graftons must be at the cantina."

"Let's take them," she said. "The odds are more in our favor now."

"I figure, oh, maybe six or seven men, counting the Graftons," Clint said. "Yeah, I think it's time to go to the cantina."

As they walked that way Clint privately worried that all of this had been too easy so far.

Too damn easy.

THIRTY-SEVEN

They reached the cantina without running into any more of Grafton's men. As they peered inside they saw Lee and Wade Grafton seated at a table. Wade looked as if he was dozing off, while Lee was staring straight ahead, a glass of whiskey in his hand. The only other man present was the bartender.

"He usually has a man out here," Clint said. "He must have sent him on an errand."

"Maybe to search for you," Scarlet said.

"Maybe. Are you ready?"

"Of course I'm ready," she said. "There's a lot of money waiting for me in there."

Lee Grafton was getting impatient. Rock should have found West by now, unless the man had left town—but why would he do that?

"I'd better get out there and see what the hell is going on," Lee said to Wade.

As he started to rise Clint stepped in and said, "No need to go looking for me, Lee. I'm right here."

"West!" he said. Behind Clint a woman entered, and Lee frowned at her.

Wade Grafton's eyes fluttered open, and the first thing he saw was Scarlet's red hair.

"That's her!" he said, grabbing for his gun. "That's her, Lee!"

"Wade, don't—" Lee said.

Wade came out of his chair, drawing his gun.

"Shit," Clint said.

"Don't, Wade!" Scarlet shouted, but there was no stopping Wade Grafton. All thoughts of greed, of getting his dead brothers' shares, flew out the window as he came face-to-face with the killer of his brothers.

Scarlet had no choice but to fire.

Her bullet hit Wade dead center this time, and he went over backward, taking his chair with him.

"Damn it!" Lee Grafton said, but he was smart enough not to draw his own gun. Instead he looked at West and said, "Who the hell are you?"

"My name is Adams," Clint said. "Clint Adams?"

Lee gaped and said, "The Gunsmith?"

"That's right," Scarlet said.

"Aw, shit," Lee said.

EPILOGUE

There were other men around, of course.

For one thing, Tucker and Lane were brought back to town by two more men after Lee Grafton had been taken. Tucker and Lane were the men who had been sent out on lookout. Only they had taken a couple of bottles of whiskey with them. When they were found they were lying on the ground snoring. They had never seen Clint, and he had never seen them.

Then there was Jeff Jacks and the other two men, who were searching the town for Clint while Sean Rock was—they thought—having his way with Juanita, Grafton's woman.

Leaving Scarlet with Lee Grafton, Clint had gone out and gotten the drop on Jacks and the other two, and they had been tied up and put in the cantina.

Clint and Scarlet decided to spend the rest of the night in the cantina with Lee Grafton tied to a chair. They did decide to remove the body of Wade, so Lee wouldn't have to keep staring at it.

Come morning, Tucker and Lane came riding in with the other two men who had been sent to find them, but they were easily handled, since they hadn't the faintest idea of what was going on. They too were tied and left in the cantina.

When Clint and Scarlet were ready to leave Domingo, Lee Grafton was tied to his horse, Wade Grafton was draped over his, and there were twenty-six men tied up and helpless—most of them also puzzled.

"Wait a full day before releasing them," Clint told Consuela and Juanita. "I don't think they'll do anything to you. They'll have had a lot of time to think things over, and I think they'll just slink away in embarrassment rather than stay around here. Make sure they know it was one man and one woman who took them all. That ought to do it."

"Do not worry," Consuela said. "There will be something else they might want after they are untied, and my girls can give that to them."

Clint laughed and said, "I'm sure they can."

Clint and Scarlet were mounted, with Lee and Wade Grafton in tow, in front of the whorehouse. Consuela waved to them and went back inside.

Juanita remained outside, her dark eyes on Clint.

"You will come back this way?" she asked. "So that we may . . . finish?"

"Perhaps, Juanita," he said, not promising anything. "Perhaps. *Adios*."

"*Adios*."

They turned their horses and rode out of Domingo, heading for the border. Lee Grafton had run out of offers of money, and threats, and remained sullenly silent.

"So," Scarlet said, "who's it going to be?"

"What are you talking about?" Clint asked.

"You've got both Angelina and Juanita waiting for you to 'come back.' Which one will you go back to when this is over?"

"Scarlet . . ."

"What?" she asked, looking amused.

"Shut up."

They continued on, both knowing that after the Graftons had been turned in and the bounty collected, what they would do was find a hotel room . . . together . . . and finish some business of their own.

Watch for

ARIZONA AMBUSH

119th in the exciting
GUNSMITH series

Coming in November!

WESTERNS!

at least a savings of $3.00 each month below the publishers price. Second, there is never any shipping, handling or other hidden charges—Free home delivery. What's more there is no minimum number of books you must buy, you may return any selection for full credit and you can cancel your subscription at any time. A TRUE VALUE!

Mail the coupon below

To start your subscription and receive 2 FREE WESTERNS, fill out the coupon below and mail it today. We'll send your first shipment which includes 2 FREE BOOKS as soon as we receive it.

J.R. ROBERTS
THE
GUNSMITH